THE
LIPPOLIK
CONUNDRUM

BOOK ONE IN
THE CONUNDRUM SERIES

BY KAMI HELM

The Lippolik Conundrum
Copyright © 2009 by Kami Helm
Cover design by Jeremy Helm

Published by:
Helm Production
215 Laura Wilkes Rd
West Monroe, LA 71292
USA

Library of Congress Control Number:
2009909156

ISBN-13: **978-0-9842287-0-6**
ISBN-10: **0-9842287-0-5**

WWW.CONUNDRUMSERIES.COM

CO`NUN´DRUM

(NOUN) CONUNDRUM - A DIFFICULT PROBLEM

SYNONYMS: BRAIN-TEASER, RIDDLE, ENIGMA

DEDICATION:

To my wonderful husband, Jeremy. Thank you for loving my weird ways and supporting me. You are my favorite person.

Also, I would like to thank my mom, Tammy and my sister, Nickie. Thank you for your wonderful ideas and encouragement. Without you, this book would not have been possible.

CONTENTS

THE
LIPPOLIK
CONUNDRUM

THE DISAPPEARANCE OF DR. CHARLES BAGBY

A fat doctor stood shaking in a garden. Above him, the bright full moon reflected off his balding head, illuminating the garden's contents. Seeing it in the moon's glow reminded him how bizarre the garden truly was. He looked around in awe.

All around him lay strange, odd-colored flowers and herbs of exotic nature and size. There were gourds and cabbages of yellow, purple, blue and orange. Fruits littered the ground as well — lumpy melons and at least three varieties of thorny plants that bore strange-looking berries. None of the plants' foreign delicate leaves had been chewed on by hungry rabbits or deer. They, too, must have been afraid to tread on such a scary, unknown world. Almost all the plants were unrecognizable to the doctor, and he was an expert at plants. He was a naturopathic doctor.

He was so afraid of getting caught that he, for a moment, forgot why he was there. The woman who owned the garden was even stranger than it was, and he was not sure what she was capable of doing to him. He was sure, however, that she would not take his trespassing lightly.

He had disguised himself, just in case she happened to still be awake. But by the loud snores radiating from inside the house, he was hopeful that it may not have been necessary. He was all in black, wearing a tight-fitting leotard, except for his shiny, white doctor's shoes, which up until now he had not thought to change. He swore at himself when he noticed them glowing in the moonlight.

He was a jolly-looking, chubby fellow, and the tightness of the leotard accentuated that fact. He sported large, rosy bulldog cheeks, which he had cleverly covered in black army paint. Under his ball-like nose, he wore a bushy gray mustache. His violet eyes were big and watery, as he searched the ground below for a certain plant in the garden. He wore a stethoscope around his neck. The doctor had grown so used to wearing it, that he had forgotten to take it off, and now the metal instrument was reflecting the moon's rays, softly. His balding head sparkled, too. With those and the white shoes, he would have been instantly spotted, if the lady in the shack were to wake. She would no doubt, be blinded by all the shine the doctor had forgotten to cover.

A look of instant dawning lit up his face, when he remembered why he had come. He needed to find a certain plant, the one that could cure the world. The doctor meandered clumsily through the strange-looking plants, quite honestly not sure what he was supposed to be looking for. The plant that he had seen earlier had been dried and crushed. This whole adventure might be wasted time. He stopped to scratch his head for a moment in thought. He wished that the lady of the house had just been a little more cooperative. If she had had any sense at all, he would not have had to do this. He was not the kind of person who went trespassing on other's properties or stole things. His mind drifted back, to three weeks earlier when he had come to her cordially.

***

His herbal supplies were running a day late, one Tuesday, when little Wayne Jones came into his office deathly ill with the chicken pox. He was in such bad shape, that without immediate intervention, Wayne might die. He racked his brain trying to think of some way to save him. Suddenly, he remembered his odd neighbor down the hill mentioning she had a garden. She had also smugly told him one day, that she "liked to grow a few remedies of her own." He would never have gone to her for help, proud man that he was; but the situation was dire, and he was out of the herbs that he needed.

He made his way down the hill to her humble shack below. His negative nature told him that she would probably not have what he needed. Upon seeing her unearthly garden up close, he smirked at his prophetic prediction and started to turn and just walk away. However, a willowy woman dressed in green striped pants and a pink ruffled blouse stopped him.

"What do you want?" she asked grouchily, as she waved a sharp shovel in his general direction. The doctor pulled at his collar uncomfortably and tried to remember what it was that he had wanted.

"Beg your pardon, madam neighbor, but I was in need of some Echinacea and Belladonna. I remembered that you had mentioned you grew remedial herbs. I had hoped you might have what I need." He looked around for a few moments, and cleared his throat, realizing that none of the plants seemed normal. "Well, I hate to have bothered you; I can see that you do not have what I am looking for. Good day, madam."

She cocked her head at him and frowned. "Who is sick, Dr. Bagby?" she asked, as if it really mattered. He was taken aback for a moment.

"Umm, well, you see...it's the Jones' son, Wayne; he's only five and already a little small for his age. He is also of a delicate nature. So, I was not surprised by how fast he has gone downhill with..." He stopped speaking, because the pretty blonde had turned around, gone inside her house and shut the door. Apparently, she had also locked it rather loudly. "Alright? Goodbye, then. Thanks for your help," he mumbled sarcastically to himself.

He turned to walk away again, when a loud, thunderous CRACK knocked him off his feet. He stood shakily, his cheeks wobbling in fear and his fists balled, searching for his attacker with wide eyes. Suddenly, the door of the house flew open. "Wayne's a good kid. Here, give him this, and he should be alright." She shoved some dried-up plants in a leather bag at Dr. Bagby.

Dr. Bagby just stood mouth agape and staring at her. "Did you hear that thunder, sir? Seems a storm's a comin'." She grinned at him and lifted a pointed finger to the clear blue sky above. Then, without what one might consider a polite goodbye, she shut the door and locked it again.

He nearly just threw the weird ingredients on the ground on his trek back, but curiosity got the better of him. When he arrived back at his office, which was also his home, he stirred the purple, crumbly mixture into a glass of water. He took a deep, nervous breath. The Jones' were waiting in the hallway lobby. Dr. Bagby carried little Wayne to his office and shut the door.

He decided to try the purple concoction, after much mind wrestling, because he had no other option. He had nothing else normal to give him, and the situation was urgent. Dr. Bagby's voice squeaked in fear, as he called Wayne's parents in to the office with them. They all watched uncertainly, as the last sticky drop oozed down little Wayne's throat. The clock began to tick loudly in his head. Dr. Bagby began to have serious guilt and doubts. Then, his fears were realized, when the boy turned a brilliant sunny yellow. Dr. Bagby's knees hit the floor. Why had he given in to that crazy woman's witchery? He put his hands to his face and began moaning pitifully, imagining the boy's demise.

His fat fingers were pried apart, however, by a beautiful, non-yellow-faced boy. "Wow! I feel great! You're the bestest doctor in the whole world!" Wayne Jones hopped off the table, and ran to his mommy. His mother stood stunned.

"You cured my baby of the chicken pox! And you did it in only three minutes! I am going to recommend you to everyone I know. That was amazing! Thank you!" Tears began to form in Mrs. Jones' eyes, as tears of relief poured down Dr. Bagby's face. Suddenly, it dawned on him. He had never seen anyone cured of the chicken pox in just three minutes. Utter shock and excitement crawled in waves down his spine, and he ran out the door.

He ran through the woods, and down the hill. His fists pounded on her door, as he stood heaving.

"Go away!" she called.

"Please, open the door. You have no idea what you did! You found a three-minute cure for the chicken pox!"

"Really?" she said sarcastically, "It usually only takes two minutes. That's weird. Okay, NOW go away."

He had to sit down and catch his breath, "That was some amazing stuff. Can I have some more?"

"NO!"

"Please let me in; I just want to talk."

"No."

"Please?"

There was complete silence.

"You could cure the world. You'd be a hero."

"I don't want to be a hero. I don't like the world."

"So…so, what??!! Wayne Jones is the only one you will save?"

"There have been others." She sounded distant and cocky.

He continued bantering and breathing heavy, but it was no use. He gave up and went away. But before he left, he made a vow to come back later and steal the miracle cure.

***

Now, here was later, a fat man in a garden poorly disguised as a ninja. He searched frantically in the dark for anything that might resemble the dried-up version of earlier. It was proving impossible. In his haste, he tripped on a large, gourd-like thing, and the flashlight in his hand flew and hit the crazy lady's door with a sickening thud. "Oh, no," he whispered.

The air became thick with electricity. The hair on his neck stood straight up. He began to pray. Then, a loud CRACK and Dr. Charles Bagby was gone. White smoke rose thickly into the air.

"Man, he was annoying!" Someone whispered behind the door.

CHAPTER 1:
THE WEDDING

The weather did not match Evy Henley's mood at all. It was quite unusual for March to have such a beautiful, sunny day. It was the kind of day people dreamed about, the perfect day for an outside wedding.

Evy had spent most of it pouting, avoiding everyone's well wishes and empty compliments. She sat under the appetizer table fuming, watching the fancy shoes parade back and forth under the table skirt. An ant crawled beside her lavender satin shoe, carrying some cheese ecstatically. Even an ant was having a good day. She squashed him with her thumb and resumed fuming.

Evy was a beautiful, twelve-year-old girl. Long red hair fell in waves on her thin shoulders. She had a pert little nose with lots of freckles. Her large eyes were an unusual shade of golden honey. The only odd feature on her lovely face was her ears, which stuck out noticeably from the side of her head. When she was little, the solution for them was a pair of pigtails, but she was long past the age of wearing those. She really did not let such things bother her anyway, because she did not worry much what others thought.

Someone hollered her name from far away. They had been looking for her for twenty minutes or so already, and she still needed a few more to calm down. The wedding could wait for her, and if it was up to her, not happen at all. Evy knew her mom wanted her to be happy for her, but she hated John, her mother's fiancé.

She wished that her sweet, innocent mother would call the whole thing off. She was making a huge mistake. No matter how many times Evy had told her how she despised him, John had snaked and charmed his way back into her mother's golden heart. Before John, she and her mother had been inseparable. She used to listen so well to Evy, but all her best efforts to talk her mom out of this were to no avail. Even her best ideas of sabotage could not prevent this day. Her mother was deeply superstitious, and Evy had even tried to create the signs that would scare her mother out of marrying him.

Her mother, Kyla, had only met this man three months ago. Her dad had died when Evy was seven, and it left a hole in both of their lives. He had been a great man. Not like John, not like John at all.

John Vespucci was a handsome, but evil, man with deep-set, black eyes. His hair was a dark, bloody red, and it hung around his face like a wet curtain. He was charming, cold, and calculating, and he definitely did not deserve Kyla's tender, sweet heart.

She heard her name again. This time it sounded more desperate. Because she was superstitious, it was a big deal to her mother to have the timing of her wedding just right. The second hand on the clock had to be in the upward position while she said her vows, or she would have bad luck. Everything traditional was kept, even the smallest of details. So, because she was worried about stressing her mother out, Evy decided to come out of hiding.

Maybe there was still time to change her mother's mind, she thought to herself. She crawled out from under the table, being careful not to soil her white hose. She stood and smoothed the front of her lavender dress, pulled a few blades of grass from her long, red hair, then snuck through the yard to the back of the house. She made her way through a maze-like sea of cats. They were strays that her mother collected. Right now, there were probably twenty of them wandering around their house. They purred as her hurrying legs brushed their soft fur.

She walked up the green garden path towards the grand, two-story house sitting on the hill. It shone, brilliantly white in the golden sun. Her mom and dad had worked so hard to refurbish it. It had been old and worn from years of neglect when they bought it. Together, they poured years of hard work into it, turning it into a radiant beacon on a hilltop. John would probably ruin it, she thought to herself.

She opened the screen door, whose rusty hinges creaked a little, but the grown-ups inside did not notice; they were busy with last minute preparations. She looked around for her best avoidance route. Everyone was so foreign to her. Most of them were John's family. Her mom had a few friends there, but only three family members, Great Uncle Woody, Aunt Penny and Big Papa. Her mother's family had always been elusive and strange, but Evy could have used more familiarity today. She found her exit and headed up the wooden, carved stairway. The light was on, and someone hummed a wedding march inside. She hesitated, knocked twice, and waited. "Yes?" someone called.

"It's me, Mom." she said feebly.

"I've been worried about you, baby. Come in, come in." Evy's mom wrapped her arms around her tightly. When she let go, the smell of her spicy perfume lingered and warmed Evy. "Well, what do you think?" Kyla asked as she turned about the room. Her hair was pulled up in a pile of loose, black curls, and her dress was a pearlescent rainbow of colors. The red ruby earrings that she always wore were dangling from her ears. They clashed painfully, but she would never take them off. She had worn them as long as Evy could remember.

Kyla looked at Evy, waiting silently. Her large blue eyes melted Evy's heart, and she lost all her conviction. Tears began to form.

"Beautiful," she whispered. She was truly glad her mom was happy, but her heart was broken for the future. She did not want to risk their relationship by ruining this moment, as hard as it was. Besides, she knew her mom had heard the speech she had prepared before.

Somewhere below, the music started. People had already been ushered to their seats. John stood tall below. His red hair was now plastered and parted against his forehead. His suit was perfectly tailored and black like his eyes. A perfect shiny smile of victory graced his freckled face. He was waiting; Evy's doom was waiting. She and her mom were to walk together down the aisle. Her feet drug a little, despite her best efforts. Down the stairs and around the corner they walked. Kyla stooped at the back door and kissed Evy's forehead. "I will always love you," she whispered. When they stepped outside, all eyes turned to beautiful Kyla and her radiance. Evy felt invisible.

The trip down the aisle was even more painful. Aunt Penny threw an over-enthusiastic grin and thumbs up at Evy, but Evy could not muster a smile back. Her mom's side was so empty, and it made her sad. Only 10 people to John's 34. In the corner of her eye, Evy thought, for a moment, that she saw a woman watching them in the woods; but she couldn't be sure. The tears in her eyes had blinded her a little, so it looked more like a blur than anything else. The rest of the wedding went horribly as planned, and no one objected. All hope of a normal life began to fade away.

Evy retreated, afterwards, to her spot under the appetizer table to cry. Uncle Woody crawled in after her and held her hand while he smoked his pipe. As weird as it was, it comforted her, and she was grateful to him for that.

The crowd thinned, and the guests went home. Her mom and John rode off into the glorious sunset, and Evy got into the car with Big Papa. She was going to spend the week at his farm in Kansas, while her mom was on her honeymoon.

When Evy eventually returned home from Big Papa's farm, the months that followed were as predictable as the seasons. By the time summer began, it became painful to watch the way John treated her mother. Kyla was strong, but distressed to find out she had been deceived by John. He was, as Evy suspected, evil and controlling.

He isolated her mother and Evy, cutting them off from all the friends and family they once knew. His inappropriate grumbles and complaints, as well as, his blatant "honesty" and bad temper, had made most of them disappear. Evy learned to avoid him altogether. She disappeared into the solace of the woods behind their house for most of the day, reading or exploring the hills. The fighting at home was more than she could bear. She saw her proud and gentle mother getting yelled at for doing nothing, and it broke her heart.

She found comfort in the trees and rivers. They were constant and peaceful. She would sit in the sand under an old oak tree by the clear swimming hole, and daydream till dark. The old oak tree became her friend, her giant shelter from the war at home.

On really bad days, it always seemed to rain. She would come home to find her mom crying. Together, they would rush through the house covering mirrors up, so as not to attract lightning. It was an old superstition. Then, they would cuddle on the porch, soaked to the bone, not saying anything at all.

But most days the sun was warm and secure, making Evy feel hope and peace. Her mom, too, kept up her happy disposition most of the time, and hoped John could change. He made a lot of promises to that effect. They were usually made, though, only after he had messed up in a big way, which was appalling to Evy. All hopes for an escape seemed elusive. She and her mom remained close, most days, conspiring behind John's back. They dreamed of the year before and held on to their past. Then, on other days, she would scold Evy for talking bad about her husband. Her mother's apologies had become commonplace and monotonous. But Evy did not blame her for her naivety back then, only her stubbornness now. It made her sad.

To add to the sadness, Evy turned 13 on May 11. Her mom's family had a weird tradition of not celebrating their thirteenth birthday. So, Evy woke up to an ordinary day, on what should have been an extraordinary one. She was finally a teenager. Her mom seemed really nervous about not celebrating it and was worried Evy would be upset. Evy could see her peering at her from behind corners and furniture all day. She did not like being spied on. She wondered why, if her mom was so worried about it, she did not change it. Her mom was extremely superstitious, though, so the tradition was going to be kept. Evy really did not mind that much. It was even kind of funny, when her mother offered her a pile of vegetables on a plate that resembled a cake at dinnertime. Her mom said it was her "un-birthday cake."

While Evy munched on a literal "slice of carrot cake," the doorbell rang loudly. She rose from the table and went to the door. A small paper bag was sitting on the porch. Evy was surprised, to say the least, at such a strange circumstance. "Who is it, dear?" her mother called from the dining room. Evy was unsure how to answer her. She opened the door and stepped onto the porch.

The paper bag had her name written in permanent black marker at the top. She strained her eyes into the empty black evening, but she couldn't see anything through the darkness. She brought the bag inside and opened it in the small hazy light of one light bulb in the washroom. Something glittered softly at the bottom of the bag. Her hand reached cautiously inside. The glittery object was hard and smooth. When her fingers touched its glossy surface, a strange sensation ran down her spine and made her brain itch. She stood motionless for a moment, wondering how to scratch her brain. The thought made her laugh. Her back was tingling, too, like little spiders were crawling up and down her spine. Evy thought it was just excitement, though, at the intrigue of such a lavish gift.

She pulled the object out of the bag. Her eyes grew large as an antique gold bracelet slid out from the bag. It was old, but had been polished with care. It had seven tiny feathers linked together with six tiny diamonds between each pair. The seventh feather in the middle of the bracelet was the largest and had an ample red ruby nestled in its center. It was beautiful. She clasped it onto her arm. A tightness in her heart loosened. It felt wonderful to get a gift. She had not realized it was bothering her until now.

She went back into the dining room. All eyes were on her as she tried to explain the paper bag on the steps and the present within it. When she raised her wrist to show her mother, her mom began to cry. Then, she ran from the table. Evy did not know what to do. John just scoffed at her. "You stole it, didn't you?" He stared her down, until she left the room.

Evy went into her room and closed the door. She looked down at her only birthday gift and smiled. Then, she took off the bracelet, wrapped it in a t-shirt, and stuffed it in the back of her drawer. She did not want to wear it if it made her mom cry.

The truth was, however, that the bracelet was not the source of her mother's misery. There were changes about to come that Kyla feared, and despite trying to make Evy's birthday non-existent, her birthday meant so much more than Evy could ever know. It was life changing.

A few weeks later, the sadness of Evy's life imploded and took hold of her heart. It was the day her mom told her she was pregnant with twins. They were truly trapped now. "Why!" she screamed, covering her mouth in surprise at the loudness of her own voice.

John's face, which had only a moment ago been full of pride and triumph, had suddenly turned ugly and glaring. "How dare you speak to me that way? You should be happy I have taken care of you all this time. You ungrateful swine! This is a happy occasion, and you will not ruin this for me."

Her mother kept her head, down lost in her own gloomy thoughts. Evy ran miserably from the house. Feeling betrayed and hopeless, she ran down the dirt road to her solace in the woods. She was crying so uncontrollably, she could barely see the road in front of her. She knew it well, though. Her feet had gone this way a thousand times before.

Out of the blue, she was suddenly hit from behind. Something had knocked her on her face in the dirt! For a moment, she did not care. She just lay sobbing on the ground, turning the dirt to mud with her tears.

But, there was something watching her. Its eyes bore into her back. She slowly raised her mud-masked face to see who it was. A **kangaroo** stared back at her! She stared back in disbelief, her mouth wide open, the mud dripping inside it. There were no wild kangaroos in America. "Where had it come from?" she wondered.

Behind her, something stirred in the woods. The kangaroo heard it, too, and cocked his head towards the sound. Then, he bolted and ran. This gave Evy even further shock, because his tail and hind end were bright purple. It was as if it had been dipped in paint. She rubbed the mud out of her eyes and climbed to her feet, just in time to see a tall blonde woman wearing bloomers dart out of the woods.

"Did you see which way he went?" the blonde asked, as if this was a perfectly normal situation. She was also wearing a bike helmet and football gear and carrying a large net. She blinked quizzically at Evy from beneath her football helmet. Evy felt like she was pointing to the left, but she was in such shock, she had done so merely out of reflex. The lady smiled mischievously, as if amused, and ran into the woods after the purple-butted kangaroo.

Evy tried to follow afterwards, but she lost them both around a hill. At least the little adventure had helped her forget about her problems. She ran her fingers through her hair, contemplating all that she had seen, and felt something tangled up in it. She pulled a large red feather out and stared at it perplexed.

The sky above her began to swirl and darken; a rainstorm began to brew. It was time to go home. Her mom was always up for a good story, and Evy could not wait to tell her. She was so excited to share what had happened to her, in fact, that she forgot about the dilemma waiting for her at home. As she ran down the road, the heavy rain began to fall.

She burst through the door, out of breath and dripping profusely on the floor. Her mom was still sitting on the couch, looking quite broken and crying silently. Evy felt the weight of her reality fall back heavily upon her. She suddenly wished she had just stayed out in the woods with her adventure. Kyla lifted her tearful blue eyes to Evy's honey-colored ones. "I'm sorry," she whispered. Evy smiled back, defeated, and took a long drawn-out breath.

"It's going to be okay, Mom. We'll be okay. Someday, I will get over it." Evy hugged Kyla hard. They sat together in uneasy silence for a while, both staring out the window at the rain pounding on the glass. "Hey, Mom. Can I tell you something incredible? I'm not sure you will believe me, but it might cheer you a little."

"Okay. Sure, baby," Kyla said, and she sat straighter in her chair wiping at her wet eyes, and trying to seem interested. She was relieved at the change of subject.

Evy swallowed hard, disbelieving it herself for a moment. "I saw a kangaroo in the woods."

"A WHAT?!!" someone snickered sarcastically behind her. In her excitement, she had failed to notice John in the doorway. "Did you say a kangaroo? I never thought you had the gumption to make up something like that just to get out of trouble." With that, he doubled over laughing hysterically in her face, which mortified her. Her mom, finding relief in the hilarity of the statement, chuckled quietly.

"Uh, yeah...I was just kidding." Evy slumped to her bedroom and shut the door. She got on her pajamas and pulled the floral covers down. She really could not blame them; it seemed incredible to her also. Loud hysteric laughter echoed in the hallway. But just before she went to bed, she stole one last glance out the window, hoping she would see a kangaroo hiding in the woods.

CHAPTER 2:

RAINY DAYS

"Hey, Kangaroo!" John called; it was his new, favorite nickname for her. He was standing outside with a shovel and a mean look in his eyes. Evy could tell he had a plan for torturing her further. It was the first time in years she had looked forward to school. The summer was creeping by so slowly, and she still had one more month of agony at home. She sighed and slunk to the door. Her mom was at the doctor's office today and could not come to her rescue. She gathered her courage and stepped outside.

"I need a hole, four feet wide and four feet deep, over there." He pointed to the far end of the yard. It was a place her mother would never see, because she hardly left the house now that her belly was getting bigger.

"And, why can't you do this yourself?" Evy asked, suddenly regretting such a pointless question before it even left her lips. John just laughed mockingly and pushed the shovel into her chest. "Does this hole have anything to do with Mom's cat, Tinker, disappearing? Because if it does, I want no part of it." Evy stood indignant.

"Dig!" John's face was bright red, and Evy knew it was best to obey before he really lost it. John was an exterminator by trade, and had a tendency to experiment his new poisons on her mom's endless supply of cats. Evy was aware that her mom knew about this, but she had turned a blind eye in order to preserve her sanity.

Evy walked to the end of the yard and sunk her shovel in the dry dirt. It was a steamy afternoon, and most of the ground consisted of clay. It was going to be a miserable job; she could tell already. The hole's size was much too big for a cat. She wondered if that was all that was going in there. John had already gone inside the house to sit in the air conditioning, but she would never have asked him anyway.

She worked steadily for hours. Sweat and blood poured from her blistered hands and dripped down the shovel's handle, making it slippery and hard to hold. She would not stop and let John see her pain, though; because he was probably watching, so she worked through it. Secretly, she hoped her mom would come home soon. John would have to let her stop once she did, for fear he would cause stress to his precious babies that she was carrying.

That was all he cared about lately. It was because he knew the power they would hold for him over her mom. It was because he thought he had her trapped. And perhaps he had. It sickened Evy to think this would be her life forever.

John returned outside with a lounge chair and a cold glass of lemonade. He wanted to watch her suffer. Her mouth was so dry; she could not salivate, even if she wanted to. The lemonade looked mighty good.

She was done digging, thirty minutes later. She marched triumphantly straight into the house, past John and into the bathroom. Once in the bathroom, though, her tears began to pour. So she locked the door and turned on the shower. She did not want John to hear her. She got into the shower and scrubbed away the tears, sweat, dirt and blood. Her hours of agony swirled down the drain. She was determined to never be left alone with that evil man ever again.

Her mom arrived home and began to cook dinner. Evy had long dried her tears, her wet hair and blistered hands were the only evidence left of her battle with John.

She tied her hair up, hiding it under a baseball cap. Then, she bandaged her hands. Then, she sunk on her bed to rest. Her mom came in her room to tell her dinner was ready. She was famished, but pretended to be asleep. She did not want to have to explain her hands to her mom.

She could hear them in the kitchen arguing again about dinner. A dish was thrown at the wall, and it shattered loudly. Kyla was crying and begging him to stop. Another dish shattered loudly against the wall. Evy could not take it anymore and covered her head with her pillow. It was not long before she was asleep for real, snoring with exhaustion and dreaming of a world without John.

When dawn broke and the sun's rays poured through her bedroom window, Evy was already up and dressed. She intended to run to the woods for a kangaroo hunt, before John could think of any more activities for her to do. Her hands hurt her something awful. She did not want to stick around to see what was going in the hole she had dug either.

In the kitchen, she snuck some water bottles and a honey peanut butter sandwich while they slept. She slipped out of the back door and tiptoed across the porch, jumping lightly to ground. She started to run, when out of the blue she heard a scuffling noise coming from the hole she had dug. Her stomach began to churn. "He's burying that cat alive!" she thought. Compassion stilled her feet, and she went and knelt beside the noisy hole.

Yellow eyes and bared teeth stared back at her in the darkness. She could barely make out the shape of a head in the dawn's low light. A loud hiss rumbled from the small creature. Suddenly, he jumped at Evy. His claws barely missed her face. A possum!

"Well, that's a relief," she thought. "I guess we still need to get you out of there, little guy." She smiled reassuringly at the still hissing possum. Before she could get to her feet, though, he lunged again. His claws fell short, luckily, but Evy could not believe what she had just seen. As he fell back in the hole, she saw that his hind end was a vivid purple, just like the kangaroo.

Her excitement built, as she hurried to John's shop to look for a box and shovel. Maybe she could catch the possum and use it as an excuse to go to the blonde lady's house. She could find the kangaroo and also discover why the weirdo lady liked to paint animal butts.

She poked some holes in the box she found and got some duct tape off the shelf. Using a shovel, she scooped the possum into the box. Then she shut the lid quickly, and taped it shut. It would not hold for long; the possum was already scratching at the walls. She would have to move quickly.

There was a small, shack-like cabin a few miles away. She had seen it on her ventures in the woods. It was the only house for miles around, so it had to be the one. She was not sure if that was the lady's residence, but it was all she had to go on. Evy took off, running clumsily in that direction. She stumbled enthusiastically down the dirt road that led to the woods. It was awkward running with such a large box.

After about a mile, the box became extremely heavy. The possum had quit moving so much, but he was heavier than a small dog. He was, she realized suddenly, the biggest possum she had ever seen. Her arms were aching terribly, so she stopped under a shade tree to drink some water and catch her breath.

The sun shone powerfully down through the trees now. Already, the world around her began to cook. It would be slow-going, carrying such a large box in such devastating heat; but the excitement of the adventure she was having spurred her on. She rose and lifted the box to rest on her hip. Evy was glad she still had the hat on from the night before. It shaded her face and kept the sun from cooking her head. That was one of the drawbacks of having such fair skin. Her head was always burning, peeling and then, adding more freckles to places she thought could hold no more. She did not like wearing caps often, though, because her large ears stuck out from her head.

She checked her bearings and turned slightly right. Up ahead of her was a large hill. Her feet found their footholds, and she began to climb. The climb to the top was steep, and she had never done it carrying a box before. Luckily, there were grooves all along that she could put the box into. It took all of her effort and a lot of her time. By the time she reached the top, her whole body was soaked in sweat and covered in dirt. That seemed to be her new look lately.

The view was magnificent from there. Small cedar and oak trees dotted the landscape. There was very little grass that was not burnt to a crisp in the summer heat, but it gave the view a raw cowboy feel. The pastures swayed like a large brown ocean in the wind. Rivers and creeks snaked their way through the hills. It was a lovely day. She took in a deep breath and let her surroundings pacify her.

She headed down the hill, now. The house was just around the other side of a cliff. Her stomach began to ache. She was hungry. When she rounded the corner, she stopped to form a spy plan and eat her sandwich. There was a small group of cedars next to a large, rock-like cliff, which gave her a good view of the shack house.

She sat the box down, which was now loudly scratching and hissing again. Then she parted the lower branches for a better view. All was quiet and still. At first glance, she believed no one was home. Then she heard faint whistling coming from a small barn next to the house. The barn looked hardly stable, as if one touch could crumble it. It was old, gray and leaning to the left. The whistling, however, was light and happy. She almost wanted to join in with the song.

Leaving the box with the possum behind, she crept in for a closer look. Evy tiptoed around the back of the shack and slowly made her way to one of the barn windows. It was hard to see in, so she had to stand on her toes. The crazy blonde lady wearing bloomers was the one whistling. She was definitely the one Evy had seen chasing the kangaroo.

She was brushing the fur of an old gray donkey with a purple butt. She had found her after all! The kangaroo was nowhere in sight, however. It felt so good to be vindicated, but she did not, however, have a good plan on how to approach them. "So... I caught a purple-butted possum. Does it belong to you?" Evy practiced and then laughed at the idea.

Just as she was working up a better story, though, Evy suddenly realized there was another person in the barn, obscured by a post. Whoever it was, they seemed to be on friendly terms with the crazy, purple-butt lady.

The crazy lady finished brushing, and sat down on a bench. "Wow, dear, does it really need to be this hot?" She remarked, wiping at her sweaty brow with a red hankie.

"Well, Aunt Myra, I am positively livid today. I know I made a mess of things, but I could really use your help. How's the plan coming?" said the mystery person behind the post. Evy's calves began to tremble with the strain of trying to stay on her toes.

"I'm still working on it." Aunt Myra sighed and put the brush down on the table beside her. "We need something discreet and safe. I'm not sure that your first plan will work now, under the circumstances." Myra pointed in the direction of the other person. The mystery lady walked around and sat next to Myra. Evy's mouth fell open, and she gasped loudly. The mystery person was her mother! The two women heard the gasp and looked straight at the window. Evy dropped quickly from their sight, just in time.

"Phew, that was close," she thought. Her heart was thumping so loudly that she was afraid they could hear it inside. A million questions swam wildly in her mind. She felt deceived and bewildered. Her mother sounded uncomfortable inside; maybe she felt herself being watched. When she continued, her voice was quieter, almost inaudible.

"I am so glad that I have someone here for me. When Evy told me that she saw that kangaroo in the woods, I just knew it had to be connected to you. You never were as discreet as you should have been." Kyla stated sarcastically. Relief flooded over Evy. She felt victorious that her mother had believed her all this time. The kangaroo was real, and she was not crazy. Who was Aunt Myra, though? And why had her mother not told her about her? There was an obvious bond between them. Part of her was glad to know there was still a part of her mother's life that she had hidden from John. It saddened her, though, to know she had been excluded as well.

Evy crept back around the house to the bushes, where she had hidden the box with the possum. The possum was the perfect reason to introduce herself to this Myra and be in on their secret relationship. When she walked around the bush, however, she was sad to find that the side of the box had been shredded open and the vital possum had disappeared. She could not show up empty-handed. It would look like she had followed her mother and spied on her. The trust between them would be damaged even more. She felt certain too that, if she waited, her mother would eventually let her meet this Myra person. So, she slunk slowly away and into the woods.

She waited until evening, sitting under the towering shelter of her old oak tree by the river. She thought about all she had seen and dreamed that this Myra person could come up with the perfect escape plan for her and her mom.

The sun began to set and Evy walked home slowly, engrossed in her hopes.

CHAPTER 3:

SIGNS

There were always signs — signs for Evy that told her she was not normal. Her mother saw them, too. She had signs of her own. Her mom's whole family had secrets, but Evy did not know them. She only knew that they existed. No one in her family was normal, so it did not surprise her that this Aunt Myra person painted animal butts. It was probably some weird superstition, because everyone in her mother's family was superstitious. Evy was beginning to be a little superstitious herself.

Although there were a lot of strange happenings going on around her lately, some signs had always been there. For one, Evy's hearing was unlike anyone else she knew. Her large ears could hear great distances sometimes and even the tiniest of sounds. Sometimes, by the river, she would sit and listen to the ants clicking away at each other. She imagined herself working as an entomologist, studying the secrets of bug language. It had become a dream of hers now.

Her mom was also getting signs — like how the weather always seemed to match her moods. She acted as if it was all coincidence, but it definitely could not be. It was just too obvious.

Evy always felt like her mother hid things from her, too. Her mother's past was shrouded in mystery, and she talked very little about her childhood. It was never a place Evy was allowed to go. Her mom's family was scattered and distant. The few family members Evy had met were kind, eccentric and funny, but never very open. They kept their distance and their personal lives to themselves. None of them seemed the least bit offended at the other's lack of personal information. There was no "how have you been?" at Christmas, just a lot of wordless hugs. Despite that, they were fun and cheerful, and she missed them terribly. They did not come around much since her mom married John.

On a happy note, however, summer was finally at an end. Evy was thrilled to be going back to school. Never before had she looked forward to her studies and the idle chatter of friends. Best of all, there was no John there to torment her. On the morning school began, she got up extra early and brushed her teeth.

While fumbling around for the lamp switch, she tripped on a homemade trap and fell to the floor. She had started laying traps for John at night before she went to bed. It helped her sleep better, knowing that he could not just walk in without her knowing. The traps usually consisted of a few upturned chairs and some strings tied to bells stretched across her door frames. She was scared to offend him in the daylight, though, and tried to remove them before he woke up. She had learned a special way to keep the bells from ringing when she untaped them from the wall.

Once all the traps were removed and put away, Evy got dressed. She had picked out a bright purple shirt, because it was now one of her favorite colors. It was the color of adventure. After throwing on some boring jeans and her old tennis shoes, she was dressed. Her mom had made wheat pancakes for breakfast. She had been on a health food kick lately, and Evy liked it. John, however, was a total carnivore, so it caused even more fighting than normal. The bus honked outside before Evy could finish. She threw one last bite in and grabbed her bag. Her mother kissed her on the cheek, and Evy rushed out the door.

The bus was mostly empty, so she had her choice of seats. She chose to sit by a seventh grader, a boy named Buddy. He had a nice smile, and she did not like to sit alone. There were not many kids on the bus or at the school, either. The town of Bluffington had a population of only three 334 people. The bus picked up several more kids and then made its way slowly to the school.

The old red school was just as cute and tiny as Evy remembered. It seemed tinier with each passing year. The building itself had only six classrooms total, one portable building and a small library. All the teachers taught more than one grade, except the kindergarten teacher. The bus driver was also the coach. The lunch lady was also the librarian. The grand total of students came to 99. Evy's classroom was the only one in a temporary building outside. Her teacher, Ms. Eldran, taught seventh and eighth grades together. Ms. Eldran was incredibly nice. She was in her late forties and had soft white hair. She was tall and elegant with almond eyes and a soft voice. Evy loved her. This was her second year with her.

The three students in her eighth grade class consisted of two girls and a cocky-looking boy. Both girls wanted Evy to sit by them, but she chose the tall skinny girl, because the seat next to her was by the window. The tall girl had her blonde hair in a ponytail, and she wore a nice new set of overalls. Evy could tell they were new, because they looked a bit stiff and they still had a tag on them.

"Hi, Evy. How was your summer?" The tall girl whispered. Evy relived the horrid moments in her mind and shrugged.

"Fine. How was yours?" And it really was fine now. It felt wonderful to be free and away from John. The tall girl's name was Adeline or Addy, and the other girl's name was Laura. The boy was James; he did not talk much. He was not happy to be back in school at all and rolled his eyes every time Evy tried to look at him.

Ms. Eldran cleared her throat at the front of the room. She waited for the room to quiet down, and then she called roll. "I would like each of you to tell me one thing about your summer when I call your name." She looked around at each student. Her gaze was intense, and she seemed to truly be interested in what each one had to say. Down the roll she called, starting with the seventh grade. When she called Adeline Reed, Addy told everyone about her splendid trip to the beach.

"That sounds magical, Addy. Okay, let's see who's next... Evelyn Henley," Ms. Eldran called.

"My mom got married." Evy said quickly, and then slumped down in her chair, not liking the direct attention.

Ms. Eldran paused a moment. "Evy, dear, that's wonderful!"

"No, it isn't," Evy whispered. Ms. Eldran ignored her melancholy statement and resumed calling out role. James barely acknowledged his name when called and only mumbled something under his breath in response to his summer experience.

The rest of the day consisted of labeling and handing out textbooks, making sure everyone had their supplies and going over the rules. The lunch bell rang at noon, and Evy was starving. The lunch room was almost half the size of the entire school building, which incidentally was not that large. It sat next to the gym. Every grade ate together at the same time, segregated to each table according to grade.

Evy sat next to Adeline and Laura. James sat on the floor in the corner, not because there were no seats, but because he did not want to sit with the girls. The lunch was a bit flat, not much seasoning, but tasty enough. Evy finished quickly. After lunch, they had recess.

It seemed a little childish to Evy that the eighth grade was to go, as well, but Evy was glad to be outside. It was a beautiful, sunny day. The sun shone gloriously above them in a cloudless sky. Everyone was running and laughing. The playground equipment was small and only for the younger kids. The big kids played dodge ball or kickball in the baseball field. Evy saw a commotion in the field and headed that way.

A large goat was standing in the middle of the field. A group of seventh graders were trying to pull the stubborn animal back into its fence, adjoining the field. It did not seem to want to go back. Ten seventh graders were apparently not enough to move him either. Coach Mims came out and gave them a hand. It was slow going, but the goat was finally placed back where it belonged. The kids cheered and got out the kick balls to play.

"He's in the field every day," someone whispered from behind Evy. She turned around to see James standing there. "What kind of lame redneck school has a goat in the baseball field?" Evy could not help but smile. Then she ran to join the game.

The rest of the day went by quicker than she had hoped. The bell rang at three o'clock. It seemed to echo in her heart, as she got a sick feeling in her stomach at the thought of going home.

The ride home on the bus was long. She was one of the first to be picked up, so she was also the last to be dropped off. Her mom was in the kitchen, already starting dinner, when Evy walked in. John had not gotten home yet; he evidently had some kind of infestation emergency at work. And Evy was able to enjoy dinner with her mom alone. She told her all about school and the goat in the field, her teacher's interest in art and how weird James was. They laughed together like old times.

The weeks at school flew by, and before she knew it, it was Halloween. She was having a grand time at school. Evy shared an interest in art with her teacher. She loved drawing and talking to Ms. Eldran about art. Ms. Eldran was even helping her learn to shade and draw perspective, if she got her work done early. That was not a problem for Evy, because the work was easy for her. It was the attention she had been missing from home.

The day before Halloween, Evy arrived at school to find that a horrible smell had taken over. Every room made her want to vomit with its intensity. Everyone was called to the gym, which luckily was not connected to the main building. The principal, Mr. Rhoades, strode sheepishly to the center of the gym and cleared his throat. He seemed a little nervous. "There has been a gas leak in the school, so school will be dismissed early today. We have called all of your parents, and the bus will take you all back home. Ummm, thanks, and have a great holiday...goodbye." With that said, he strode out of the gym.

When Evy arrived home, she found John in the kitchen talking on the phone. He laughed mockingly at someone on the other end. "I told you to leave this to a professional, Mr. Rhoades. I think I would know better than you how to clear up this issue. The original price still stands. Well...do you want me to help or not...I knew you would come to your senses, so to speak! Senses, get it...oh, man, that's funny. Alright, I'll take care of it. Bye." John hung up. He seemed in good spirits about the conversation he had just had. He pretended not to notice Evy's arrival, which was an improvement. Kyla toddled into the room. She was getting so big with the twins now. The doctor had told her she was having boys. This, of course, pleased John to no end.

"What was that about?" she asked. John smirked and pulled a chair out. He sat down and put his feet up on the table. "Mr. Rhoades, the principal at the school, turned down my reasonable offer the other day. He has since changed his mind." John seemingly wanted to draw this triumphant story out as long as he could. "He thought my prices were too steep. You see, the school had a skunk infestation. He thought he would just deal with it himself. He crawled under the school last night with a rifle and tried to shoot them." John could barely control his laughter. His face was as red as his hair. "Well, he got two of them, but the little boogers let loose such a smell, it took over the whole school, which is why little miss prissy here is home early." He gestured to Evy, finally acknowledging her presence. "Apparently, my price is now a reasonable one. I need to go take care of the rest of them this weekend."

Evy was upset that John had already started causing problems for her at school. If the principal felt cheated or humiliated, she would pay the price. There was no escape from him, it seemed. She shrugged off her worrisome thoughts and decided to concentrate on her costume for Halloween. John had refused to buy her one, but her mom had an old sewing machine that she had inherited from her grandmother. They were working on some costumes together. Evy was so happy to have a project to do with her mom.

Hers was supposed to be a scarecrow. She had gathered some of her old clothes that she had outgrown and cut them into pieces. She then stitched the patches together, so it looked like an old quilted shirt. She found an old hat at a garage sale and glued dry grass to the inside brim. She decided to wear her old pair of jeans with a few sewed-on patches as well. It was turning out pretty great.

Her mom had decided to be a pumpkin. She had an orange shirt that was big enough to fit her belly, and she had drawn a happy pumpkin face on the front. They were both excited about Halloween.

Evy, however, was excited for a different reason. She had a plan to meet Myra. She decided that, while her mom and John were out at a Halloween party, she would go to Myra's house. She had convinced them she was going trick or treating with Adeline, so the plan was formed.

While she was sewing her costume, Evy was suddenly overtaken with an emotion of anticipation about taking her twin brothers trick or treating someday. It hit her by surprise, because she had not thought about the baby boys in this light before. She was suddenly hopeful at their coming. She told herself to make sure and tell her mother how she was suddenly looking forward to their arrival.

She had resented the idea of them for so long, and she needed to be a great big sister for them. She decided to change her attitude at least about them. Her mom came into her room to see how the costume was progressing. Evy struggled to thread a needle, so her mom took over.

"Mom, all this Halloween stuff has made me think about how fun it will be to be a big sister. I am so excited to have some little brothers." Evy felt the knot in her stomach subside a little. Her mom seemed speechless and hugged Evy so tight, it choked her a bit. Evy thought, for a moment, it might be an opportune time to bring up Aunt Myra, but decided against it.

She wanted to go and spy on her again, study her in her strangeness. Her mother had still not mentioned her at all, and it was beginning to frustrate Evy a little. That is why she made up her mind to go and speak to her herself.

The next evening, her mom left at six o'clock with John. Kyla wore her pumpkin costume and her giant ruby earrings that did not match. John wore only his normal attire. Evy waved them onward and rushed inside to get

her supplies, which she had stashed earlier under the bed —
a flashlight, rope, pocket knife and some water.

She pulled on some heavy boots and started to walk
out the door. She paused and looked at her dresser in front
of her. The top drawer was open. She was worried John
had taken her bracelet. She reached into the back of her
drawer and pulled out the wadded T-shirt. She unwrapped
it and found the bracelet still inside. Relief flooded over
her. She put it on her wrist for fear that John would come
and take it away. Then, she headed out of the house. She
decided to hide the bracelet somewhere better later.

She was in costume, of course. She had to wear it;
she had worked so hard on it. The shirt was quilted in
different materials and had hay glued in small holes she had
torn. She had also glued hay in the sleeves, so that it would
hang out. She painted a scarecrow face on with her
mother's makeup.

She was going to knock on Myra's door and say
"trick or treat," of course. It was her plan. Never mind that
Myra's house was in the middle of the woods. That was
only a slight setback and no one would truly go there just
for candy. She started down the dirt road toward the hills.
Her flashlight flickered, leaving her afraid in all the small,

completely dark moments. Her mind wandered with only the crickets to talk to. She wondered if a friendship with Myra could begin, and if it would lead to freedom from John. She felt hope begin again.

She stood at the base of the hill where she had climbed before with the possum, collecting her courage as it ran from her once again. She was not sure how to approach climbing in the dark. Unfortunately, the moon was shrouded in clouds. She used the rope from her bag to tie the flashlight to her head. It was crude, but it would work. She found her hand-holds and started up. One foot slipped and rocks tumbled down below. She moved the unsupported foot to another hole in the rock and started again. She slowly made it to the top. At the top, Evy untied her rope helmet from her head, placing it back in her bag. Her flashlight was very dim now, and she wished she had changed the batteries before leaving.

Around the corner, Myra's rustic house came into view, barely visible in the trees and darkness. The lights were not on in the house, and Evy was praying she was not asleep. She crept loudly across crunchy leaves toward the door. She could hear heavy snoring coming from the barn, but it was not a human sound. She raised a shaky fist to the peeling wooden door. Three loud knocks that could have woken the dead echoed loudly in the valley around her. Evy could hear loud mumblings from inside; someone seemed pretty annoyed. The mumbling got louder and closer. She began to think that this was not such a good plan after all. Then the air around her felt suddenly hot and she felt the hair on her neck stand on end.

"Trick or t…" Evy had barely whispered the words, when, suddenly, she felt hot electricity running through her whole body. A loud BOOM cracked overhead. There was not time to scream; it was over in less than a second.

Evy lay dazed and smoking on the ground. Her head hurt badly; and she couldn't see very well, because she was dizzy. She felt someone, probably Myra, drag her by the leg to the barn next to the house. She felt…odd. Her body felt lighter and smaller. She could hear voices above her arguing in the dark.

"Oh, no! Myra, not another one! This one looks so young. Oh, this is terrible." The deep, soothing voice of a man sounded sad and frustrated.

"I know." This time it was Myra's voice; Evy recognized it from her previous trip.

"Who is it?" the man asked.

"I'm not sure, because they were disguised. Sound familiar?" She paused sarcastically, as if making a point.

"She's waking," the man whispered.

Evy's eyes opened slowly. Her head was still hurting terribly. The smell of burnt feathers permeated the air.

CHAPTER 4:

A DUCK AND A SCARECROW

Evy blinked and stared up at two pairs of gawky eyes. Myra and a donkey stared silently, anticipating a reaction of some kind. The man whom she had heard earlier was nowhere in sight.

Evy lifted a shaky hand to her forehead, only it was not a hand, but a feathery wing that touched her forehead. It took a moment to register, and then Evy let out a horrid scream that echoed throughout the entire barn. Her whole body was covered in feathers. Her feet were yellow and webbed, and her feathery butt was a vivid purple, like the other animals she had seen. Her head feathers, however, were dark red. She was in utter shock. Then without even a second thought, she rose effortlessly and began flying in circles around Myra and the donkey's heads. She was a duck! A duck! "How did this happen?" she quacked.

Faster and faster, she whirled about the barn in a panic. And then she realized she was flying, and that sent her into a totally different sort of panic. Unexpectedly still, one of her duck feet turned back into a human foot, which made her fly lopsided, because of the weight. Around and around she flew, quacking at the top of her now small lungs. She circled, screaming in her duck voice for an hour until her voice finally went out.

Tired and defeated at last, she landed awkwardly, heaving to the ground. She crumbled into a mass of feathers and began sobbing. Myra just sat down on some hay and watched, but the donkey came to sit beside her.

"There now, don't cry. You'll be alright." The soothing voice of the man she had heard earlier flowed from the donkey's lips. It was just one more shock she had not anticipated, and it made her cry harder. She cried for the longest time, and Myra seemed to be getting fidgety on the hay. Her thin gown was not thick enough to keep the hay from poking through it and making her behind itchy.

"Enough crying," Myra said dryly. "I'm getting annoyed, again."

"Well, we don't want that," the donkey replied sarcastically.

"Like it really matters now. Although, I do feel sorry for the poor thing, seeing as it did not change all the way. Look at its foot," Myra sneered back.

Evy's tears began to lessen. She did not feel like crying anymore. She was angry now. "What did you do to me?" she screamed. She had never felt so angry before. It pulsed in waves down her spine, and she felt it trigger something deep inside. Her body began to shake and change. One wing popped out and turned back to a human arm.

Myra stood so suddenly that one of the curlers on her head flew off. "Did you see that, Dr. Bagby? First her foot and now her arm."

The donkey smiled and leapt in the air. "She is fixing herself. How did she do that, Myra? Ask her how. I have to know!" He pranced and leapt some more, which was a pretty funny feat considering his size.

"Why can't you ask me yourself?" Evy sneered. Although, she really was not sure how she had done it.

"WOOHOO! She can hear me!" The donkey jumped higher in elation, kicking his feet in the air. "Maybe I'm changing, too. Maybe that's why she can hear me." The donkey was beyond ecstatic.

"You look the same to me," Myra said coolly. But there was a little disappointment in her voice.

Evy was not sure how to feel now, but she could not take the suspense any longer. "Will someone please tell me what is going on?"

"Oh. Umm, well dear, the thing is… You're a duck." Myra had only stated the obvious.

"And how am I a duck?" Evy seethed between her clenched duck bill.

"Well, it's complicated." Trying to get information from this woman was like trying to get cheese away from a mouse.

"Uncomplicate it, please." Evy tried not to sound as angry as she felt. Apparently, it was a bad thing to annoy Myra.

Myra plucked a long chin hair from her chin and rubbed the sore spot thoughtfully. She was unsure how to go on. Although she had had this conversation before, it was never an easy one. She really hated being scratched, stomped and kicked, which seemed to always be the consequence of such a conversation. She began, a little robotic and rehearsed.

"I am sorry for your troubles. I didn't mean to turn you into a duck. Oh yeah, and please don't run away, because I will have to catch you." She paused dramatically and waited, letting it soak in a moment. "I turn people into animals when I am annoyed." Evy still sat silently staring and waiting for more. "Umm, this is the part where I usually say, 'I'm sorry, but it is a permanent change; and I'm the only person, to whom you will ever be able to speak to,' but I'm not sure that applies here. I'm not sure how you changed your arm and foot. That's never happened before."

Evy's mind tried to process what she was saying, but she felt suddenly afraid. Another wave of emotion washed down her spine, and she felt her head tingle; her ears popped back on. Myra could not help but burst into laughter. She laughed partly from the intensity of the moment and also the absurdity of the situation. Not to mention, Evy looked incredibly silly. Dr. Bagby was happy as well. Every fiber in his body hoped that there really was a cure for Myra's terrible ability. He watched her intensely, hoping to learn the secret of how she was changing back. She was surprised that he was not taking notes. Evy was not sure what to think. She was still numbly shocked. Her thoughts were beginning to get a little clearer, but she still felt like she was dreaming. She began to try and clear her mind, and perhaps figure out how she was doing this. Maybe she could turn back completely. She could not stop her brain from running over scenarios, however, where she would be stuck as a deformed duck forever.

Suddenly, a hideous thought occurred to her. It was a terribly, sad realization about the possum, the donkey and the kangaroo. She realized suddenly that they had been people — people who must have crossed paths with Myra. The thought made her incredibly sad. Once again she felt the waves of that emotion wash down her spine, and her other leg popped into being. Myra and Dr. Bagby said nothing at all. They just sat and watched her like it was some freaky TV show.

Evy was starting to feel a huge amount of anger towards Myra. She did not want to like her anymore. She was a monster! She realized, at last, why her mother had kept her from her. A huge bolt of anger exploded inside of her and her whole body began to tremble. She felt herself changing yet again. Pop! She was totally human, dressed as a scarecrow, once again. She lunged at Myra, knocking her off the hay bale she was sitting on. Myra eyes grew wide from shock, but she did not have time to ward off the attack. Evy pounded Myra in the chest with her fists over and over. Myra tried pushing her off, but Evy was determined.

Dr. Bagby he-hawed loudly behind her in vain. His voice was no longer human to her, now that she had resumed her normal status. He finally lifted her off of Myra by biting her shirt with his teeth. Myra sat up and brushed the straw and dirt out of her hair; all of her curlers had been strewn around her in the mist of the ordeal.

Myra was seemingly unsurprised by the absurd situation. She acted as if it was just normal behavior to be attacked by a scarecrow-turned-duck-turned-back-human in the middle of the night. Myra lifted her dirty body off the ground and brought the lantern that was hung on the wall closer to Dr. Bagby. Her face was covered in dirt and there were tear drawn trails down it. She sniffed and then leaned wearily on Dr. Bagby's massive shoulder. "I'm getting too old for this, Bagby," she whispered. Dr. Bagby nodded sympathetically.

Evy's anger was subsiding a little. She sat down on some hay and sighed deeply, going over her options carefully. When she finally looked up at Myra, the light of the lantern caught her face, and Myra gasped. "Evy! What are you doing here? I didn't recognize you before. Oh, what a silly statement that was. Of course, I didn't recognize you. First, you were a scarecrow; then, a duck, and now a scarecrow again. Oh, I am so glad you inherited your Grandmother's trigger. How lucky is that?" She smiled but only by herself. No one else understood her blathering speech. "Oh, for Heaven's sakes, Your Grandmother Evelyn was a shape-shifter...like you, apparently. If only we had not both lost our jewelry...Didn't your mother tell you?"

Evy sat in stunned silence listening, but not hearing or understanding any of what Myra was saying. Her arm burned hot beneath the bracelet on her arm, and she rubbed it absent-mindedly.

The phone rang loudly from the house far away. Myra seemed annoyed, and it was worrying Evy a little. Her muscles tensed in preparedness for a flight far away from her, just in case.

"I'll be right back." Myra said and left swiftly from the barn toward the house.

Evy sat perfectly still. She felt so confused. There were so many questions and thoughts in her mind. Why had her mother kept something so huge from her? She still felt sad for the people Myra had changed. She wondered how many there were. Dr. Bagby seemed to have learned to cope with it. She wondered why he stayed. She had so many questions! Evy was not sure if Myra was a danger to her or not. She did not know how she had turned back to herself again, and she did not want to risk being stuck as a duck forever.

After about five minutes, Myra returned with a rotten leather book under her arm.

"Evy, that was your mom. She was worried and couldn't find you. I told her you had come here...but, let's keep the whole duck thing to ourselves, shall we?" Evy nodded in fear. It sounded more like a threat than a suggestion.

"Well, if I can trust you with this book, I will let you borrow it. It has photos of your family in it. I can't reveal much, that's your mom's job. Perhaps now, you should start asking your mom some hard questions. Anyway, I told her you were on your way home. Dr. Bagby will allow you passage on his back, until he feels you are safe. I hope you don't stay mad too long. I would like to get to know you better. Perhaps, we can meet under more acceptable circumstances next time."

Myra threw a red checkered blanket on Dr. Bagby's back. A doctor's stethoscope hung from the hook where the blanket had been. It had obviously been there a long time, because it was rusty and cracking. She wondered how long Dr. Bagby had been changed. She pitied him and therefore, was not afraid to climb onto his gray, hairy back for a ride home.

There just so happened to be a dirt road leading around the back of the hill and around to the highway towards her house. It was a fact that could have saved her the trouble of climbing the steep side of the hill. She made a mental note and then sat back to enjoy the slow clip-clop of the donkey's hooves on the hard, rocky road. You could tell by the look in the old donkey's eyes that he wished with all his heart to talk to her on their journey home, but alas, he could not. It saddened Evy immensely. He had such kind violet eyes. They said so much to her, even in their silence, and she missed the sound of his soothing voice.

Her porch light was on in the distant darkness. The donkey stopped far enough away that he would not be seen. Evy slid down his side to the ground. She took out her flickering flashlight. Her eyes met Bagby's; she smiled and thanked him.

"I will come to see you again, but next time I won't come alone. There's safety in numbers," Evy laughed. Her laugh surprised her, because it was a happy one. Even though it had been a scary adventure, she felt elated at the changes that she knew now would come. She was special, and she was determined to learn more. She hugged the donkey doctor, and then headed home with the rotten leather picture book hidden safely under her scarecrow shirt.

When she entered the house, her mom greeted her at the door. John stood behind her watching. "It was so nice of Adeline's mom to drop you off. We were out so late and when I called, she was so kind about offering to bring you home," Kyla winked at Evy as if to say, "We will talk later."

"You can tell us all about it in the morning. Off to bed now." Evy was thankful and weary. As she passed John, however, he reached out his arm to block her way. Fear gripped her for a moment, and she felt her spine tingle. This tingle she felt, after tonight's events, could definitely be a bad sign.

Then he lifted his other hand to the top of her head, and pulled a long red feather from her hair. "That is so interesting," He said mockingly, "I've never seen a feathery kangaroo before." He sniggered at his own joke. Evy rolled her eyes and headed to her room. The feather from before, however, the one she had pulled from her hair after seeing the kangaroo for the first time, suddenly made sense.

In her room, she pulled the leather book out of her shirt and tucked it under her bed. Then she washed the makeup from her face and put on her pajamas. She carefully set up her traps: the upturned chairs, the bells on strings and the hairspray on her nightstand, just in case. With the traps set, she fell peacefully asleep.

In the morning, she quickly and quietly undid all the traps and got ready for school. Her mom had unexpectedly fixed her lunch. It was sitting on the counter next to John's, with her name written in bold letters. The bus honked, and she grabbed the lunch bag and ran to the door. "I love you!" she called, but her mom was nowhere in sight. She shrugged it off and headed to the door. She had tied the red duck feather to her backpack, so that she knew for sure that last night had actually happened. Besides, it was part of her, and she did not feel right just throwing it away.

A slight rotten egg smell still hung lazily in the air above every classroom. Tomorrow was the weekend, though, so Evy was hopeful that by Monday the smell would be gone.

School was uneventful, until lunch. When she opened the brown bag her mom had packed for her, a note was inside. She unfolded it carefully and began to read;

"My sweet baby girl,

I was so worried about you last night! I wish you had told me that you were going to her house, or that you even knew about Myra. I should have guessed you would figure it all out, what with the kangaroo and all. Myra's never been very discreet and you're so smart. I don't know what she told you, but we definitely need to talk. I am going to go and visit her this morning to try to get some ground on what you know. I will find a way for us to be alone today to talk.

I love you always,

Your Mom"

Evy's excitement was uncontainable, and she let out a small squeak right in the middle of the cafeteria. Everyone started laughing, but she did not seem to care.

She became immersed in her own thoughts and totally forgot about eating.

CHAPTER 5:

VANISHING

When Evy came home from school, the house was empty and cold. Dropping her backpack in the washroom, she went to her bedroom. She had hoped to find her mom waiting there to answer all of her thousands of questions, but there was no one home. Suddenly remembering the leather picture book tucked under her bed, made her quicken her steps.

She rushed to her room and fumbled beneath the bed. Her fingers traced its cracked peeling surface, and she gathered it slowly into her arms. She always wanted to know more about her family. When her father died, she had lost so much of it. Tears of anticipation and relief came to her eyes. She did not want to rush into this, but to savor every photograph on every page and touch them lovingly.

Inside, there were a lot of old gray photos of a man with a long beard, wearing overalls and the biggest smile Evy had ever seen. She knew exactly who he was. She loved his smile. It was Big Papa. There was a photo of a younger him in an officer uniform, shaking the hand of someone who looked important. There were a few of him with his family. He stood lording over his small wife and their four kids, two boys and two girls. He was a giant of a man. Below the pictures of him, were the words "Big Papa" written appropriately.

She also recognized a much younger Uncle Woody, standing tall beside Big Papa, looking up at him proudly. Myra was also in the photo holding a small girl on her lap. She only knew it to be Myra, because the title said it was her. The tiny mother of the children held a baby, known as "Jacky" in her arms. The photo looked really old — older than Myra could possibly be. Evy wished her mom was here with her to help explain this all to her.

There were lots more photos of the same family throughout the years. Myra began to look more recognizable the older she became in the photos. The younger sister of Myra looked a lot like Evy's mother. Her name was written below her photo, as "Evelyn".

Evy gasped. It was a photo of her grandmother, her namesake. If Myra was correct, then she had also inherited more than just her name. She had inherited her "triggers", as well, whatever that meant. The events of the last couple of days seemed so unreal to Evy. The thought of herself as a duck sent a shiver and goose bumps down her arms.

The last few pages were of her mom as a baby, nestled in the arms of her grandmother. Evelyn was smiling adoringly at baby Kyla, and a proud daddy stood behind her. She wondered what had happened to her grandfather. She had never known him. His face was strong and kind.

There were a few pictures of Kyla as a toddler, usually accompanied by a dog who was sitting happily next to her. She figured out that the dog was of a magical nature, because the paws were strangely a dark hunter green and Myra had told her that her grandmother was a shape-shifter.

A normal person, however, would have chalked the photos up to mean that the child was an animal lover, but Evy now knew the dog must have been her grandmother changed to an animal. She wondered why there were so many of her in an animal form and no more as a human. Evy had never gotten to know her grandmother. She wondered what had happened to her. She also wondered if her whole family had gifts. So many questions filled her mind; her brain ached from the pressure of them.

The front door creaked open loudly, and Evy could hear John fumbling with something heavy. "Evy!" he bellowed. "Come help me with this!"

Evy pushed the book she was holding back under the bed and willed herself to obey. She could see that whatever it was he was carrying was larger than she was. Upon closer inspection, she realized it was a large cage probably intended for the skunks at school. She struggled under the weight of it, but helped him drop it in the living room, a place she knew her mom would strongly disapprove of. John sat on the floor next to it to examine it further and figure out a plan. Evy slipped out of the room un-noticed and un-thanked. She turned on her radio and shut the door, waiting on pins and needles for her mom to return.

Her mom was gone for hours; so, Evy knew there would be a fight waiting for her when she returned. John was never nice if he was hungry. She was hungry, too. So, she decided to go get a snack. Somehow she made it to the kitchen without John noticing. It was probably because he was enjoying the terrible ideas he was coming up with for those poor skunks. She made herself a sandwich and looked out into the evening dusk for some sign of her mom.

Far away in the distance, she saw her mom's car coming slowly up the dirt road. The car seemed a little anxious about getting to the house. It was probably because it knew what awaited it. Evy's sandwich caught in her throat and choked her with fear, where once excitement had been. Try as she might she could not swallow it, and she threw the rest away.

To her utter shock, John never noticed her mom walking in the door. He was going over school blueprints, enthusiastically. Every once in a while a large crooked grin would show up on his face. It was the only true smile of happiness Evy had ever seen him smile.

Kyla motioned Evy to her bedroom and shut the door, heaving a sigh of relief. "I thought surely I was in for a fight." She turned on the light and sat on the bed slowly, gripping the bottom of her belly and lifting it, so her knees would not knock the babies. She sat on the bed breathing heavily for a moment, not sure where to begin. Evy could not wait any longer. She did not want the idol chit chat that would inevitably come first, so she skipped to the point abruptly.

"Mom, do we have super powers?" Her mom flinched slightly at her boldness. She had waited so long to tell Evy, that it had become a secret of sorts. She still felt as if the subject were off limits.

"Not, exactly. There is so much to tell you. We have to keep our voices down, though. You may ask anything you wish. I will try not to overwhelm you. I want you to be ready, not afraid. Let me begin with a story about your great Granddad. You know him as Big Papa, but his real name was Maurice Lippolik." Evy's face lit up at the mention of his name.

"Maurice Lippolik was born in Ireland. He was the youngest of ten children, seven boys and three girls. He was the seventh son of a seventh son. There is an old superstition that believes that particular birth order to be significant. It is said that the seventh son of a seventh son will have special powers. It's true.

He came to the United States at age five to live with his Aunt Mary, who was a very odd and deeply superstitious woman. When he turned 13, he realized he had the power to heal other people. His Aunt who had been very sick for a long time was cured suddenly, by what she described as, 'blue lightning that came from Big Papa's fingers.' He grew up in North Carolina infamously and was married to a girl, who he met in Ireland, while visiting his family. Her name was Shannon. She was a gorgeous, red-headed woman with a deep-bellied laugh.

After college, Big Papa worked for the President of the United States. It was before he had children. No one in the family was sure what he was doing there, but we all believed it had something to do with his power to heal. He was a great man, the kind you knew you could trust with even your greatest secrets.

One sad day, however, he came home from working overseas for a few months. He was a changed man. He was still a good man, but he seemed distracted and worried. He packed up the house, and they moved far away from Washington. He never told us what happened. Grandma Shannon noticed a giant pendulum hanging around his neck with strange writing on it. When she asked him about it, he told her he had gotten it from an old lady in Ireland as a gift. He never took it off after that, and he would always hide it in his shirt if we asked about it.

The next week, he found work at a lumber mill. Things went well for awhile. They were happy, and soon they found themselves parents to four wonderful children. Big Papa worked at that mill for 13 years. Then, one day he came to work, to find that they were laying off workers at the mill and that Big Papa was one of the ones to be fired. This upset him greatly and he began to cry.

He was a very decent and caring person (don't make that face, Evy). Anyway, as his tears hit the dirt floor of the mill, small trees began to grow from the teardrops. He did not notice this at first and continued crying for a while. Pretty soon, there were small trees growing rapidly inside the mill. They grew so fast that they destroyed the building they were in. It collapsed. Luckily, everyone was unharmed. The next day, as expected, the government showed up and took over the mill. None of the workers really knew what had happened, so Big Papa was never found to be responsible.

The family packed and moved again. This time Big Papa became a farmer so he could use his "triggers", as we came to call them, appropriately. He still lives on a prosperous farm to this day, which has not found its equal.

I remember Momma telling me, that on their thirteenth anniversary, Grandma Shannon found a beautiful brooch made of pearls and diamonds in the shape of a rainbow lying on her dresser. She refused to wear it. In fact, I don't think she ever took it out of the box. She thought that Big Papa should not have spent so much money on her. She was a very practical woman. Big Papa, however, insisted he did not buy it. Grandma Shannon died way before you were born, but they would argue every anniversary over that stupid brooch.

Pretty soon his children began to display "triggers", as well, when they turned 13. Each of them, just like you, received a piece of jewelry in a paper bag delivered to them mysteriously. 13 is such an unlucky number. I knew this was coming. That's why I watched you so closely that day on your birthday. I guess I should have warned you, but how do you bring up that conversation? It was better for you to figure it out alone, and then talk to you about it after. It is out of my hands now.

The bracelet you received will always remind you that you are different, just as these ruby earrings remind me. I was shocked to see it and to realize that you, too, would possess powers. I am pretty sure that Big Papa sends the jewelry. He denies it, however. But where could he have gotten his medallion? We all think he has a treasure trove hidden somewhere. I have tried to find out, ever since I received my gift.

It is such a thoughtful thing that he does, though, and you should wear it with pride. It is the only present a

Lippolik gets for their thirteenth birthday." Kyla looked lost in her thoughts for a moment. Then she continued.

"The Lippolik family's special powers manifest, or are triggered, when they get emotional. For example, to make the plants grow tall at harvest, Big Papa would tape pictures of his children as babies to the front of his tractor and then cry all over that field. He would drink gallons of water and by the time he got finished; he was totally dehydrated," Kyla laughed, "It brings new meaning to the term, 'he built his farm with blood, sweat and tears,' doesn't it?

Each person triggers on a different emotion. For Big Papa it was sadness. For Myra, it is irritation. For me, for some reason, it is all emotions. I can change the weather to fit my mood. I'm not sure what your powers are. I must admit I am curious, but we Lippoliks do not pry.

Myra gets her green thumb and her healing power from Big Papa, also. I wish I had her healing powers, because they keep her young and healthy, they are the gifts of life. As for her other triggers, well...she is not the only one who has struggles with their emotional gifts." She laughed again. "So...you are a Lippolik; it's that simple and yet that complicated. I would rather John not know, and I am sure you would, too. Any questions?"

Evy sat in silence, letting it all soak into her mind. It was overwhelming and scary.

Her mom looked at her puzzled. She was worried that she might have said too much. "All you have to do is learn to control your emotions. You will have to discover you triggers on your own. Just try not to do that in front of anyone, okay? Your life will be seemingly normal that way."

"I'm hungry, woman!" John yelled from the living room.

Kyra struggled to stand, and Evy helped her to her feet."I told Myra we would visit together tomorrow while John is working at the school. We will talk more then."

The next morning, Evy awoke dreary and tired. She had barely slept at all. So much information had been crammed into her head at once. The old leather picture book lay open on her chest. She had spent hours during the night scanning every picture for clues. She did not want to miss anything. Every face on every page was now familiar to her. She was also wearing her beautiful bracelet once more, having been given permission. She reveled in its splendor. Its carvings were so intricate and graceful. She wondered who sent it to her and why.

John was already gone, when Evy made it to the kitchen. His steaming plate of wheat pancakes lay untouched on the table. Evy could not eat after others or she would have loved to save her mother the trouble of making her another plate. She felt a little guilty about her squeamishness. Her mom made her a plate, anyway, and then fixed her own. They sat together in silence. Evy felt like she had never truly known her mom. So much was hidden from her all her life. She could tell her mom felt uncomfortable with her secret revealed, because she barely ate. The weather outside was as unsure as Kyla was. The overcast sky covered the sun's luminous rays with a hint of rain that was indecisive to fall.

After breakfast, Evy helped clean the kitchen and then stood and waited by the door. Her mom concerned herself with silly things to try and avoid the trip to Myra's. So, Evy waited. She waited while her mom changed her shoes twice, made the bed, dusted the curtain and took out the trash. On the way back in from taking out the trash, Evy shut and locked the door in her face with her mom's purse on her shoulder. She guided her to the car.

"Mom, let's go. I am so ready for this." Evy coaxed her with a smile. Her mom tried to smile back, but it was clear that she was afraid of the truth.

It was such a short trip to Myra's in a car by way of the road. It made Evy laugh to think she had worked so hard to get there before. She was arriving this time minus the sweat and dirt. She was moving up in the world. When they got to Myra's, her mom hesitated to get out of the car, so Evy just went to the door without her.

Myra was sitting on the porch reading a true crime novel. She lowered her book, but did not put it down. As Myra's eyes moved to Evy's face, Evy flinched involuntarily at the memories of their last meeting. A wave of anxiety went down her spine. She felt her body changing once again, out of fear.

"So…we know you can become invisible, too. Huh?" Myra acknowledged the obvious. Sure enough, Evy had turned invisible. Her mom bolted from the car in a panic.

"Myra, what did you do?" Evy's first reflex of worry began to subside and her body fluttered back to visible again.

"That was awesome! I was scared Myra would turn me into a duck again, and I turned invisible. How wicked cool was that?!" Myra winced at the mention of the duck, and waited for an imminent explosion.

"A duck?! When did you turn into a duck? MYRA!!" Kyla's face turned beet red. Evy's did, too, because the look that Myra was shooting her made her very nervous, and it was causing her to become invisible again.

"It's no big deal. She isn't one anymore, so let's just move on. So... how are you feeling today, my dear?" Myra tried to change the subject, but Kyla just stood fuming on the porch. Her large belly and red face made her look almost comical. The clouds over their heads were not funny, however, as they began to darken and swirl.

Myra panicked and tried to grin at Kyla to console her, a feat that she had obviously not done in awhile, and so consequentially, was very forced and scary-looking. Her face was stretched tight and her teeth were forced together in what seemed like more of a grimace, than a smile. It was such a funny sight that Kyla and the ominous clouds began to calm.

"You're very lucky that Evy's okay or I might have had a few electrical shocks of my own to deal out to you." Kyla hissed.

Myra's face looked a little scared and her hair stood straight up with static electricity, a sign that she was feeling a very real scared emotion. Kyla waddled to the wicker chair next to Myra and heaved her plump behind into it. Evy who had stood motionless for more than five minutes watching the strange fight between them in fear, finally let the rubber legs under her win out and sat down hard on the porch. Silence followed for a while. They all just sat staring into the cold, winter forest. An owl who-whoed quietly in the boughs of a nearby tree.

"So... how did you get away from John's watchful eyes?" Myra asked, breaking their silence at last. In the distance, Dr. Bagby walked slowly into the woods chewing on something green. He had a large, red quilt tied around his middle with a rope like a makeshift coat.

"He had to go and exterminate some skunks up at Evy's school this morning, so we just got lucky." Kyla replied and seemed to relax a little, but Myra sat up suddenly.

"Oh, no! That's where Clarence is!" Kyla's face became instantly white.

"Why is Clarence at the school?"

"Who is Clarence?" Evy asked feeling lost.

"I sent him there to keep an eye on Evy at school. I never thought that he would be in danger there." Myra and Kyla just ignored Evy's question.

"Well, John usually likes to bring home his victims, once he cages them and try out his new poisons at home. We will just have to free him, before he can do Clarence any harm," Kyla plotted.

Evy shouted louder this time, "Who is Clarence?!" Her sudden outburst made Myra jump, and her hair got all static again.

Myra just sat in wide eyed silence followed by a frown. "I don't really feel like company right now, all of a sudden." She stood and walked to the front door, pausing a moment to kiss Kyla on the cheek, a little too hardly. Then she shut the door and locked it loudly, causing a lucky horseshoe to fall off its hook above the door, barely missing Evy's head.

Kyla shrugged at Evy, who stood with wonder at Myra's odd ways. "Come on dear, we need to save a skunk." They walked away together and got in the car headed back home. "So...who is Clarence?" Evy asked, much more meekly this time.

"He was a blind date with Myra that went terribly wrong back in college. He started out okay, but his breath stunk horribly the whole date, which of course, annoyed Myra immensely. Surprisingly, he was not that mad when she turned him. He was happy to still have an excuse to hang around her, because as it turned out, he liked her a lot. She uses him to spy on people sometimes. They've become pretty good friends, kind of like Dr. Bagby, too. Although, I think Dr. Bagby sticks around because he is waiting for a cure to pop up. I'm not really sure."

When they arrived home, John's car was in the driveway. Kyla looked worried. Evy could see John in the living room window lying on the couch. "I will go in and distract him, while you go let Clarence out of the cage."

Evy nodded. She knew that the cage would be in John's shop. He had had a hard time fitting it in the door last time, even with Evy's help. She wasn't sure how to get the skunk out, though.

"You know that invisibility thingy would come in handy right about now," Kyla added, looking hopeful.

"I'm not really sure how to do that again," Evy said, smiling awkwardly.

"That's okay, sweetie. We'll just have to do it the old fashioned way, without triggers."

Evy and Kyla got out of the car. Evy waited outside, while Kyla went inside. She slumped down, and moved quietly towards John's shop, which was connected to the house on the front. She could make out a small hairy figure huddled in the darkness, inside the cage. She fumbled for the light switch and switched it on. The flickering light revealed a small, cute, purple-butted skunk, shaking terribly inside the large cage. At the site of Evy, he perked up his head and jumped with delight.

A loud fight broke out inside the house, and Evy knew there was only a little time left to save him, before John needed some torturous stress relief. She looked around panicked for the key, but could not find one. Her eye caught sight of a large pair of wire cutters on a work bench.

She worked feverishly to cut the wire, and the skunk stood clinging white-knuckled to the bars of the cage, looking worried. "Don't worry Clarence we will get you out of here."

The last of the wire was finally cut, and she dropped the wire cutters noisily. They fell clanging to the ground. Unfortunately, they clattered louder than Evy had anticipated on the concrete; it sounded like thunder echoing off the walls. She could hear silence follow from inside the house.

"What was that?" John asked. Evy scooped the skunk into her arms and hurried out of the shop door. John was coming! She could hear his loud stomps coming towards the door.

She raced around the side of the house and headed to the woods, just as the door of their house flew open and John bellowed. He was fumbling clumsily after her, his face turning bright red and his long legs dangling like streamers behind him. Kyla waddled as quickly as she could after him.

Dr. Bagby emerged out of the woods ahead of Evy and she ran to him, glad for such a lucky happenstance. She put Clarence on his back and clamored up behind him. Bagby's face looked frightened at the sight of the clamoring, furious John headed towards him. He turned back towards the woods and began to trot.

John, upon seeing Evy riding away, grabbed a shovel and a bicycle from the yard and pedaled furiously after them. A look of terror contorted Bagby's face, and he began to run faster. But, John proved pretty nimble through the cactuses and small cedar trees. He followed closely with a wicked grin on his face, swinging the shovel in the air. "I will get you for this, Evy!"

A wash of panic flowed down Evy's back, causing a deep reaction to bubble inside of her. "Oh no!" She thought.

The clouds over their heads began to turn black with menace, and she heard Kyla scream, "Leave my baby alone!" A giant bolt of lighting zoomed brilliantly from the sky and hit behind Evy, followed by a huge clap of thunder.

It was all too much for Evy, and she felt herself triggering. Her whole body began to shake. The path in front of her began to blur and melt. Dr. Bagby and Clarence cried out suddenly, in apparent pain. They stopped running, too, because they had hit some kind of invisible wall. A feeling of cold weightlessness enveloped them like jelly and suspended them in midair.

Evy's body was so still and light, as if only a shell of itself. Dr. Bagby and Clarence, too, were as still as death. She was relieved to feel them breathing heavy, though, because it meant that she had not killed them.

Then, there was a bright all engulfing light; she began to plunge. She clung tightly to Bagby's makeshift, quilt coat. She fell fast and hard, meeting the ground with crushing pain and then darkness.

CHAPTER 6:

COFFEE AND KIWIS

She felt cold. Her face and everything else hurt terribly. Evy awoke from her nasty fall to find that she was face down in the dirt. Her head was throbbing, which made her vision a little blurry. Thoughts of John's malicious chase never entered her thoughts. She was too concerned for her pain. It was hard for her to breathe, also. She hoped that her ribs were not broken. Her breaths felt heavy and thick like there was hardly enough oxygen to please them. There were moaning noises coming from behind her, too. She rose, shaking, up onto her elbows and turned her head. Bagby and Clarence lay sprawled on the ground, also. She stared at them a second, trying to remember what had happened.

Then suddenly, it all came rushing back like a freight train. She remembered that she was on the run. Evy panicked, stood quickly and turned around. Her chest was heaving in fear and her spine was tingling painfully. But, John was not there. She ran breathlessly through the trees looking for her mother, calling her name. She tripped on an old bicycle lying hidden, half buried in dirt. The bike was burnt, black and rusty. She pondered it a moment, it looked like John's. Evy gathered herself again and ran to the clearing in the woods. There was no sign of her mom.

Atop the hill, where her white house should have been there was nothing. The whole house was gone. It had vanished. She ran to where it used to be and tried to feel for walls or a step…anything. She had hoped that maybe it was just invisible or something, but it was completely gone. Where was her mom? She did not understand what had happened. She was able to stay mostly calm, because of what she had been through and seen — so many strange happenings lately. There had to be a reasonable explanation. After much thought, she decided to head to Myra's house, maybe her mom would be there.

She walked back towards the dead winter woods, biting her nails and wondering what was going on. Clarence was awake and had climbed on Bagby's head. He had his tiny, pink, skunk fingers wrapped around Bagby's big ear, and he was chattering into it in tiny clicks and whistles. Bagby did not stir. He looked badly hurt.

Evy kneeled beside him. She picked up his large donkey nose and laid it in her lap. His warm breath brushed the hairs on her arm.   He was barely breathing. Evy rubbed his soft nose and then laid it carefully back on the ground. She rose to her feet.

"We need to go get Myra. She'll know what to do." Clarence nodded. He climbed up her leg and onto Evy's shoulder. He smelled awful. She had to fight the urge to vomit, but she did not say anything about it. She walked quickly through the woods, keeping her eyes open for signs of trouble. It was afternoon now, and she would have to be quick if there was any hope of bringing Myra back before dark.

They walked swiftly and made it to Myra's house in good time. Evy approached it carefully, though. If she had learned anything out of all her misadventures, it was not to spook Myra with sudden movements. Loud humming was coming from inside the house. She knocked on the door and waited. A loud shotgun-cocking noise sounded from behind the door, "Who's there?" Myra hollered daringly.

"It's me, Evy," She said and waited impatiently, frozen from the chilly winter wind. She hated being left outside. She wished she could just walk in and there would be no secrets on the other side, no hiding, no danger.

Myra opened the door and peered out of it with her eyebrows furrowed. At the sight of Evy, her eyes widened and she took a step back. "You're alive?! Thank God for that. We wondered if you were okay. Why do you look the same? You still look 13. Are you a ghost? No matter, I could use some company." She opened the door wider and bid them come in. Evy took a deep breath; it was suddenly easier to breath inside Myra's house. "Is that you, Clarence? I never thought I would see you again." Clarence reached out his tiny hairy arms for a hug, but Myra just turned around and headed to the kitchen.

Her house was tiny. It was just one large, very crowded room. There were newspapers stacked half way up the walls and large gaudy knickknacks everywhere. It appeared that Myra was a bit of a packrat. Her house was crammed full and laid out into four designated areas or corners.

There was one overstuffed, flowery couch in what must have been the living area, along with a cheerful little, black stove glowing in the corner. A flat, lacy, lopsided bed, lay in the far right corner and a small, messy kitchen was piled in the back left corner. A wooden dining table stood in the front left-hand corner, and it was so covered in objects that she could not determine its true shape. Dried herbs hung in curtains all over the ceiling. Large live plants lined the walls, too, in potted jars, which were placed precariously on the stacks of newspapers and books. There was not one spot of free space. Even the walls had pictures hung side by side. It was truly a chaotic way of living.

"Myra, Bagby's hurt and he won't wake up. I can't find my mom, and my house is missing!"

Myra turned around from worrying over the kitchen stove that would not light, to look at Evy. "Bagby's with you?" Her eyes looked misty. She rubbed the wetness from them and then turned away again, busying herself with something at the counter.

"Okay, well, that's a lot to handle. Let us do one thing at a time, shall we? Evy, be a dear and bring me that dry Gumlily on your right. It is the dried, yellowish root. Yes, yes...that one." Myra grabbed two more dried plants from the wall and began to mince them. She added some water to the bowl and mashed it all together to form a paste.

Then, she stepped backwards and aimed her pinky finger at the bowl. A tiny, purple lightning bolt shot out of her finger and lit the contents of the bowl ablaze in purple flames. A huge thunderous CRACK resounded inside the house. The floor boards and pictures on the walls shook violently. Dust, dried petals and leaves fell in showers over their heads.

Evy nearly jumped out of her skin, and Clarence squirted out a terrible cloud of stink into the air. "Wow! That was crazy loud. What did you do, Myra?" Immediately, Evy's nose wished it could retract into her face as Clarence's putrid odor found its way inside it. "Clarence...why?! That is awful. Don't you ever, ever...again."

"Shall we go then?" Myra asked impatiently, once again ignoring the obvious oddness of the situation. She did not appear to care much about her outrageous triggers shocking others. She was who she was. Evy was not sure if she liked that about her or not. She might have respected her more for her pluck if she had not turned her into a duck. Myra had not been too sympathetic or apologetic afterwards either.

Myra wrapped a few odd-colored scarves around her throat to ward off the winter chill, tucked the bowl under her arm and strode out the door with Evy at her heels. Evy had to run to try and get ahead of her, but Myra never slowed down. They strode quickly through the brush and cactus, Myra's bright colored scarves blowing behind her like flags. She surprised Evy by making it down the side of the hill with no difficulty. She never acted as old as the picture book must have been. Her healing powers had made her stay young and healthy. Evy directed her steps from behind.

They found Bagby much the way they had left him. He lay barely breathing and sprawled awkwardly on the dusty road. Tears welled in Myra's eyes when she saw him, but she quickly wiped them away.

Myra raised her hand and slapped the donkey hard across his face. Bagby startled, he hollered loudly and kicked his legs out in self defense. Luckily, no one was standing close enough to get kicked. Myra did not wait for him to compose himself before she began mashing on his body. She pulled and pushed different body parts, trying to see where he was hurt. As soon as she touched his ribs, he screamed. It almost sounded like a woman's scream, and Evy had to stifle a laugh.

"Oh hush, don't be a baby," Myra said, but could not help but smile a little. She enjoyed his discomfort. It was only fair to her that he suffer a little after all the suffering she had been through lately. "You have some cracked ribs," Myra stated. Then she dipped her fingers into the paste that she had made prior and spread it over his wounded side. The medicine glowed faintly; already, it was apparently making the pain of breathing easier for Bagby.

He rolled onto his good side and struggled to stand. It took a few minutes and all the others just watched him. They would have helped had he not weighed a literal ton.

It was beginning to get dark. The last pink rays of the sun streaked through the sky, turning the winter woods into a glowing wonderland. The four of them made their way slowly down to the dirt road in silence. Although the road was longer when walking it and not driving, there was no hope of a donkey climbing a steep cliff. Evy was relieved that they were all safe, though. She hoped and prayed that her mother was, too, wherever she was.

She waited till they got to Myra's house to ask about her mother again. It was very dark by then, and the frozen winter chill had begun to creep in out of the trees. Everything was so quiet that it unnerved Evy.

Usually, even in the winter, the woods were buzzing with life and noise. Tonight there was only silence beyond the whistling wind through the branches. She was afraid to ask the question that had haunted her all day. They reached Myra's house already blanketed by night. Evy sat on the porch, while Myra took Clarence and Bagby to the barn and made them comfortable.

Myra returned to the porch where Evy sat wrapped in an old quilt she had found. "A couple of warm blankets and a good night's sleep, and Bagby should be alright," Myra said, but she seemed a little broken as she said it. Her eyes were puffy and red. She stared at Evy a long time with them, looking for answers. Evy stared back, because she needed answers just as much.

Evy had found that having powers was not as great as she had imagined it would be. She wished she could just go back in time with her real dad and be happy and normal again. She wished that her wonderful dad had never died and then everything would be okay. She felt herself starting to cry, but she held it back. This caused a painful lump to form in her throat and her spine to tingle. She turned her focus instead to Myra.

"Where is my mom?" The words were choked and barely whispered. Myra looked at the ground and then reached her hand out to Evy.

"Come inside and we will talk. It's getting chilly out here." Evy hesitated a moment and then rose to her feet, ignoring Myra's outstretched hand. She did not trust her still, and from the tone Myra chose, the news must not have been good.

It was warm inside. The embers of the fire from the small black stove sparkled and spit. Myra walked into the kitchen and lit a pilot on the stove. It roared to life easily this time. She dipped water out of a bucket on the floor and poured it slowly and carefully into a teapot. She was very careful not to spill a drop as if it were more precious than gold. She placed the teapot onto a burner, and then grabbed a kiwi out of a bowl of fruit on the counter. She began to peel the fruit, which was surprisingly bright red inside. Evy shoved some things off of a chair so she could sit at the table. She waited patiently trying not to annoy Myra, but Myra seemed lost in her thoughts anyway. It was beginning to annoy Evy, instead. She wanted to scream "Out with it!!!" but she did not.

Myra took a deep breath. She waited a moment to set the stage and then she said, "Evy, I haven't seen or heard from your mother in over two years."

Evy's mouth flew open. Of all the words Myra could have said, she had not expected to hear those. "What do you mean, you haven't seen her in two years?! We were just here this morning!!"

Myra made two cups of coffee. She brought them, along with the sliced kiwi to the table. She did not bother to move the junk off of the chair; she just sat on top of it. She cleared her throat. "I have not seen you for over twenty-five years, Evy. That morning was a long time ago. We were so worried about you. You just disappeared. It broke your poor mother's heart in two."

"So, what exactly are you saying? I don't understand. You're talking like a loony person!" Evy was close to tears now. She had hoped to find good news about her mother here, not more insanity talk. Myra looked rather calm in the midst of such a life changing speech and it was making Evy very angry. She felt a trigger roll down her spine, and her hands began to grow long, fingernail-like talons. Her body began to sprout red feathers, too.

Myra panicked and tried desperately to calm her. "Please, let's just talk about this! It isn't my fault, just calm down. Good gracious, you don't have to get so dramatic all the time." Myra's hair was standing on end, also and purple lighting was spouting from her fingertips threateningly.

Evy realized that she should calm down and let Myra explain. She took some deep breaths and her feathers dropped one by one off of her body. Her nails shrunk slowly back to normal.

Myra sighed deeply and sat back in her chair with her legs crossed. "Now, that's better. Let's try this again, shall we?"

Evy tried to relax also, but could not get comfortable in the hard, wooden chair. Her mind was stressing over what she might or might not hear. She wiggled this way and that, until Myra grabbed her by both shoulders and forced her to sit upright.

"As I was saying, dear, you disappeared twenty-five years ago. We thought you had just turned invisible or something to get away from John. But, when you were no longer in danger, we expected to see some sign from you. Some little sign that would say you were okay. We had hoped that you might simply calm down and reappear. We hoped and prayed for days, in fact, which turned into weeks and then eventually years. Your mother never gave up hope. ('But I did,' Myra mumbled) She sat for two days on her front porch, just waiting for you. I tried to get her to come inside and out of the torrential rain, but she wouldn't. She was devastated. Finally, she finally came inside, but she wouldn't lock the door. She left it open, in case you came home. I thought that you died after about a week, but your mom wouldn't hear it.

Then, the twin boys were born in February. They were beautiful babies. Kallon, the oldest, had dark, black hair like your mom and black eyes like his dad. Bowen had auburn hair like you, and blue eyes.

Right away, Kallon showed signs of his father's personality, though. It made Kyla so sad. He was so awful to his little brother and beat him up all the time. He experimented on and tortured your mom's cats with the poisons he found in his father's shop. He got into the shop by learning to pick locks. Bowen would try to save the cats, but he was so much smaller than Kallon. He was not able to. Kallon also struggled in school and did not listen to his teachers.

Bowen, on the other hand, was all the goodness his brother was not. He was kind and sweet. He could charm the socks off of anyone. He was funny and entertaining, while Kallon sulked and kept to himself.

Kallon grew jealous of his brother's attentions. He would lock Bowen in his father's shop all the time after school. Your poor mother wasn't there to stop him, because she had to work. Since John was gone..."

"Where is John?" Evy asked. Myra just waved the question away and continued.

"Since John was gone, your mother had to work to support the boys. I helped as much as I could, also. One day, after the boys had had their thirteenth birthdays, she returned home from work to find Bowen almost dead and lying on the floor of the locked shop. Kallon was in his room playing video games. Kyla frantically unlocked the door and called 911. She confronted Kallon about his brother, but he said that he did not know what had happened to Bowen. Kallon said, he must have locked himself inside the shop and then hurt himself. He had a smirk on his wicked little face the whole time.

She begged and pleaded with him to tell her what was wrong with Bowen. She screamed and reasoned. Meanwhile, Bowen lay still as death, pale and green on the floor. The ambulance arrived and whisked Bowen away. A police inquiry began. They concluded that Bowen was poisoned.

Since Bowen was not able to tell them how he was poisoned, because he could not remember, the police decided it must have been an accident. But Kyla knew different. She had a horrible feeling that Kallon, Bowen's own twin brother, was responsible. So, she shipped Bowen off to live with Big Papa up in Kansas. Just to keep him safe.

She tried her best to whip Kallon into shape. Big Papa came down for a month to help, leaving Bowen at home to recover on the farm. He spent hours giving strong, manly advice to Kallon about morals and values. Big Papa tried to spend time with him fishing and hunting, but Kallon was too far gone. When all of their efforts did not work, they sent him to military boot camp. They had hopes that it would straighten him out. They thought that it would soften his bloated ego, but unfortunately, it only made him stronger. He became a nightmare.

He had so many people fooled, too. He only let a few people know the true him. He was forever angry that his father was gone and that Bowen was the favorite. He learned his triggers without guidance or want of guidance. He used them for his own glory.

He joined the military right after school, and did despicable things while he was a soldier. He rose in power and rank. When he came through the war, he was a decorated hero, falsely so though. His medals were given to him for things he never did, but claimed to. People were too afraid to cross him. He loved the attention!" She paused and looked at Evy's empty cup. "Oh, would you like some more coffee, dear?" Myra reached for Evy's cup, but Evy just shook her head, entranced with the story.

"Okay, where was I? Oh yeah, so... he came home a hero. He was far from it though in reality. Once he was no longer in the military, he got bored and restless after a few months. So... he decided to destroy the very country that idolized him.

He broke into Big Papa's house and stole Bowen's thirteenth birthday jewelry. Then, to add to that disgrace, he dug large holes all over their farming land, searching for treasure, with help from his hooligan friends. Big Papa cried so hard that a large oak tree grew two hundred feet in their backyard in one day.

Then, he took over the country. I still don't know how he did it, but it was a brilliantly evil plan, because it worked. No one would believe you then, either, if you had told them it was him.

Everyone thought he was a hero. But, I knew him as a child, I was afraid of him even then. There was something very evil and wrong about him. There was something dark, way down inside his eyes, which took your very breath away." Myra shuddered visibly.

"Wait. I'm so very lost. This whole story sounds a bit bizarre. AND, where exactly is my mother? Are you ever getting to that answer? DID you say that he, my brother Kallon, destroyed America?! My head hurts..." A shaky hand rubbed at her forehead. Evy felt sick and weak inside. The outlines of her body began to wave, she was turning invisible.

"Evy, I don't know how to tell you any other way. Your half-brother, Kallon, killed half of the people in America and the animals, too. He poisoned the water, somehow. The plants are the only things that seem to be adjusting. A lot of trees died, but some of them are coming back and seem to be immune now. The air is hard to breathe, though, from lack of oxygen. Look, I know it was him!

On top of that, he has declared himself the King of America. He has taken over every state with his Snake Pirate soldiers, and if you don't join him he will poison your water. It's some kind of a sick, twisted, terrorist takeover. He was too fast and too cunning to stop. By the time anyone realized what was happening, it was too late. One drink, one shower, one time washing your hands, was all it took. So many people died within seconds.

Your mother left to try and stop him two years ago, and she disappeared. I have been left here alone for far too long. There hasn't been anyone to talk to in years. So, if I sound crazy, it's probably because I am." Myra took a deep breath and looked Evy over once again, as if to affirm her existence. She thought for a moment that she might have been having some kind of crazy apparition, imagined to fill the void in her loneliness. "Would you like some more coffee or kiwis?" She asked again. Evy stared at her blankly, totally in shock.

"Well, if you don't believe me...here." Myra reached over to a dusty stack of newspapers piled in the corner. She grabbed three of the top ones and shook the dust and cobwebs off of them, then handed them to Evy.

The first one's headlines read, <u>Dead Water</u>. The story was about not drinking the water from certain river regions. "..Thousands have drunk their last drink and washed their hair for the last time...a massive evacuation is the only answer...scientists baffled..." Another paper read, <u>River Terrorists?</u> It showed pictures of dead animals and trees, barren wastelands, people traveling in groups and living in tents. The third newspaper was the most disturbing of all. It was a picture of a young handsome man, who looked a lot like John, wearing a comical crown and seated on a lavish throne. The title read, <u>The King of America!</u> The story spoke of Kallon's war heroics and all the medals he had won. It heralded him for his bravery. Then, it said that he could save everyone. That, he was working on an antidote for the poisons in the river. He was said to be, "a savior of the people".

A tear ran down Evy's face. "I have to go back and fix this," she whispered, but in truth, she did not even know how she had gotten here in the first place.

CHAPTER 7:

THE KING OF AMERICA

King Kallon Vespucci squirmed uncomfortably in his plush, green chair and rubbed his fingers over a giant, green ring on his right hand. Stone-white skeletons lay scattered about his lavish chambers. He stared at them with pleasure and counted them over and over. They were like twisted trophies to him, reminding him of his great power. He was extremely bored, though. He could only count bones so many times.

An ugly, gray molting possum lay dozing at his feet; its buttocks were a bright, purple color. The King kicked the possum awake and gestured for a crow-looking girl in the corner.

"I'm bored! Go tell Rufus, to look me up some trouble." She walked over to the possum who was still massaging his sore purple behind. The skinny, crow girl bent down slowly and whispered into the possum's ear. Rufus the possum sat up straighter, his eyes glowing wickedly. He rubbed his little possum hands together, and grinned mischievously. Then, he ran full sprint down the

THE KING OF AMERICA

long, graceful palace hallway. If there was trouble to be found, then Rufus would find it.

He had a bone to pick, anyway. His first stop was always his sworn enemy's house, Myra Lippolik. The King was never interested in trying to do anything about her, though. He had misplaced loyalty to his family. But Rufus had hopes, that eventually, he could turn the King on Myra. So, she was always spy stop number one.

It was a long ride to Myra's house, two hours in fact, by car and gasoline was getting harder and harder to come by, what with the country half dead and all. There was no talking Rufus out of it, though. He was the King's favorite pet of sorts, so no one questioned him. He was probably the favorite, because his hatred was as great as the King's and they both had a passion for stirring up trouble. The crow girl was Rufus' translator and a cousin of the King. Her name was Gracie; she sat beside him always. His driver had been with him a long time, too. He was a giant brute of a man who never spoke, so they worked well together. They knew his routine, so they began without a word.

Rufus danced excitedly in his seat for the whole two hour trip. He squirmed and hissed, singing loudly in his squeaky possum voice. Oh, how he enjoyed misery! Gracie could not take it any more, and she put her headphones on.

It was perfectly dark when they arrived. It was better that way, for a possum and for a spy. They pulled onto a dirt road about a thirty minute drive from Myra's house. The tires crunched loudly and a hazy cloud of dirt rose to tree level. A large barn loomed in the distance and lit the way. It glowed like a beacon, and to Rufus, represented vengeance in every way. Any person who might have stumbled across this particular barn might have been shocked to see its contents, even repulsed at times.

The car came to a stop and Rufus got out. He was the only one allowed inside, and he did not need Gracie. There were large, purple letters above the door; "Welcome to the P.B.U. Pub." Rufus knocked four times. A small wooden door opened and a large eyeball peered out into the chilly night air. "Password?" someone bellowed in a deep roaring voice.

Rufus hissed excitedly, "Purple Butts United." The small door was slammed shut and the wall of the barn slid open, just enough for Rufus' small form to fit through. He walked in regally, because here he was the king.

It was smoky and dimly lit inside. There were purple-butted animals everywhere. The majority of which, were white sheep. They were playing cards at long tables and lounging in soft chairs smoking cigars. A kangaroo was standing at the bar in the back, pouring drinks. A black horse with her horsy lips painted bright red was singing on a stage built of hay. A few of them were playing darts with a large blown-up picture of Myra's face. A small white Chihuahua sat in the back watching everyone and chewing tobacco. She had paws that were green and a purple butt, too. There were probably thirty or more animal morphs there, encumbered together in one common hatred of Myra.

Rufus strode to the stage and attempted to climb up the lady horse's back to get to the mike, but she kicked him off with a snort. The music stopped suddenly. Rufus picked his sore body up off the floor, and rubbed the hay out of his fur. He pointed a scrawny finger heinously at the horse. She just strode off the stage in a huff; her big, purple behind swaying rhythmically. Rufus ordered a pair of pigs to bring him a chair. He climbed the chair instead, so he could reach the mike, "Attention, fellow P.B.U members, is Gus here yet?"

The whole room was silent; curls of smoke filled the awkward air. The bartender kangaroo put down the glass he was cleaning and pointed to a set of stairs that led to the loft above. "Thank you," Rufus said dryly. He climbed down and bounded up the stairs toward the loft. The black horse trotted back on stage and began singing again.

The loft was all aglow. Bright computer screens filled the whole room with light. The screens were all pointed at various places inside Myra's house and yard. They were spying on Myra at every angle possible. There must have been five in her house alone. A few more surveyed the outside of her home and two more inside the barn beside it.

Rufus' eyes glowed with excitement when he spotted the donkey and skunk sleeping soundly under a tattered blanket in the barn. "New recruits," He mumbled, smiling at the armadillo sitting in front of the screens. "Good evening, Gus," Rufus slapped his old friend on the back of his shell. "You did a good job setting this all up. Now, we can keep an eye on enemy number one at all times. How did you pull it off?"

The old armadillo smiled and introduced Rufus to Twinkle and Bob, two white mice with glowing, purple butts. "These two little guys made all this possible, along with about two hundred old car batteries."

Rufus nodded gratefully to the pair of mice and saddled up in a chair beside Gus. Together, they sat silently watching. Myra was in the kitchen fixing a pot of coffee. Then, she carried the cups and a plate of fruit to the dining table, where she sat down across from a red-haired girl at the table. About two minutes later, Rufus hollered, "What's this?" nearly falling out of his chair. "Can you zoom in on the dining room area? Is that? No, it couldn't be. Did you see that, Gus? Tell me I'm not imagining this."

"No sir, I saw it, too," Gus stammered. "Let me get that tape, so we can watch it again to make sure."

They rewound the tape and watched with anticipation. The girl that was sitting at the dining table with Myra morphed into a bird creature with red feathers, and just as quickly, dropped the feathers off her body and turned back into a human. Rufus was in shock. He sat down and rubbed his eyes with his paws. "Play it again."

So Gus did. When it was confirmed what he had seen, he asked to see it again.

It was so unbelievable. Part of him felt that he had seen this girl before, too, but where? "The King will be very pleased with this Gus. I am sure, he will be as interested as we are, to learn this girl's secret. I will take it to him right away. He might be so pleased, in fact, that we might finally have our revenge on Myra."

CHAPTER 8:

DEAD WATER

A cloud of soft, twinkling dust bunnies swirled and danced on Evy's sleeping face. She lay bundled in an old quilt on Myra's fluffy, floral couch. Her long eyelashes fluttered softly, scattering the sparkling dust and causing it to swirl upwards into the bright streams of morning sunrays flowing from the window. She opened her eyes widely, a look of panic frozen in them for a moment as she forgot where she was. She sat up suddenly and looked around. Reality fell hard on her mind and memories returned, crushing her once again to the heart.

She yawned and stretched. Her bare toes reached nervously towards the hard, cold planks of the floor. She winced as the icy cold inched up her leg when her toes hit the floor. She felt numb and sad. Her mother was gone. Where was she? Was she even still alive? She sat for a moment on the couch too weary to move as she scanned her surroundings.

Myra must have gotten up already, because her bed was made and she was nowhere in sight. Evy rose from the couch. The long T-shirt she had borrowed from Myra to sleep in hung past her knees. Evy's coat was hanging by the front door and her clothes where scattered on the floor. Her shirt had a big, muddy boot print on it.

A brisk draft was grappling at her from under the door, and Evy shuddered when its cold fingers touched her. She pulled on her pants and socks. Her boots were nowhere to be found, however. The house was so cluttered, but yet oddly neat. It was as if the piles of junk were piled into massive, chaotic categories. Finding her boots would be like trying to find a needle in a neatly organized haystack. She put on her coat and began searching for her boots. She found one under the couch, but could not find the other. She resigned to her fate of one-booted-ness and limped crookedly out of the front door.

A blast of cold air hit her squarely in the face when she opened the door, and she took a step back. The sun was shining somewhere far away, but it was through the veiled clouds. Dead trees and hard, dirt ground lay before her as far as she could see. Even the grassy fields beside the woods were bare. She missed the soft sway already, the comfort of the waving sea of them. She closed her eyes so she could run through them in her mind. But everything was dead. Tears filled her eyes. She never thought that she would ever be in this spot or in this time, so alone.

Myra's faint whistling was coming from a small chicken coop next to the barn. Evy's heart leapt for joy when she spied the garden still growing beside her. Somehow Myra had kept it alive. It gave her great hope. Myra emerged still whistling out of the coop. She looked up and smiled at Evy, waving her hand for her to join her. Evy hobbled over to Myra. Myra looked down at Evy's one boot.

"Ooooh, here you go, sorry..." Myra handed Evy her other boot, now filled to the brim with chicken eggs. Evy glared at her. "Come on, pick you out a pumpkin, and I'll make us some pumpkin muffins," Myra said cheerily.

Evy walked sideways down the gardens deep trenches still wearing one boot. She did not have the heart to dump out the eggs. There were no "pumpkins" that she could find, however. There was something that resembled a pumpkin, but it was bright, yellow and square. She shrugged her shoulders and lifted it from the ground, snapping it off the vine. It was larger than Bagby's head and heavier. Evy carried it into the kitchen and helped Myra make the muffins.

It comforted her to do mindless work in the kitchen, but her mind mulled over its stresses anyway. The decision she came to was an easy one. She was going to go and find her mom.

After breakfast, Evy and Myra took warm muffins out to the barn for Clarence and Bagby. They were already up and brushed clean. "Myra must have come to see them earlier," Evy thought. Bagby's side was dyed purple where Myra smeared the medicine on him the night before. Evy waited till Bagby had had his tenth muffin and Clarence was still working on his one muffin, and then, she cleared her throat.

"I'm leaving today to go find my mom. I just know that she would want me to come and find her. I know that it is dangerous out there right now, what with the evil King and all, but I can't stay here and do nothing. I'll need your help to prepare, but I would like to get going as soon as possible. My only other option is to try and go back, but I don't even know how I got here. My trigger was fear, I think. Maybe someone should try and scare me terribly."

The barn was silent. No one moved. Clarence choked a little on his muffin. Myra stared at the floor for a moment, tracing her toe in the dirt.

"I'll come with you to find your mom," Myra said, not raising her head. "I should have gone after her a long time ago. I should have gone with her, actually. I helped raise her. What kind of person just sits back for two years and does nothing? I'm coming."

"Me, too," Clarence chimed in for only Myra to hear. It just sounded like squeaks to Evy.

"Alright, I guess I am, too, then. I can't really stay here alone, can I?" It sounded more like a question than a statement from Dr. Bagby, and Myra gave him a heated look.

"Well then, there is much to prepare. Come on, Evy. I'll need your help to pack."

Clarence clamored after them without an invitation. Inside the house, Myra pulled an old suitcase out from under the bed. It was covered in dust, but was already packed full of clothes. "I've meant to go after her all this time," Myra said sadly. "I guess I just needed a push." She grabbed a rainbow woven bag off her headboard and began stuffing it with various objects.

"Evy, go and pack the food, dear. I'll take care of the water issue, there is a method that I use...There are muffins, bread, dried apples, a bag of oats and some canned goods. I think we can hitch a small wagon onto Dr. Bagby. Clarence, go and fetch the tent out of the barn. I will get some blankets. We can put those in a trunk."

They all worked silently. Evy went out and found the wagon. The wheels were rusty and squeaky, but it was good enough. She filled it with all the food she could find in the kitchen. Clarence drug the tent to Evy, which took some time, and she placed it carefully on top of the food supplies. Myra emerged from her house carrying the suitcase, the woven rainbow bag and a big glass water jug with a large, purple flower floating inside.

"This is a hybrid of the Hyacinth Eichhornia Mycelium. It is how I have survived all this time. I've always had rough well water. I was able to combine these plants with some other useful variants, and now this flower cleans all the toxins out of the water, including whatever the King is putting in it. I call them H.E.M.I.s: Hyacinth Eichhornia Mycelium Improved." Evy nodded, extremely impressed.

Bagby was bundled once again in his makeshift coat. He had ropes tied in knots around his neck and chest and then tied to the wagon. Myra tied two glass water jugs in baskets and then, strapped them across his back, one on each side, each one holding a precious purple H.E.M.I. flower.

After Myra scattered enough chicken feed for the hens to last them for a few days, she wrapped her many scarves and a thick jacket tightly around herself. They were ready to go. Clarence bundled himself in a quilt that was lying on top of the tent and bags. The other blankets were placed in an old trunk, which they put on the back of the wagon. He was already sleeping.

"It could be a long way from here walking. I don't have a clue where we are going, either," Myra said, rubbing her cold hands together to try and stay warm. She stole a longing glance back at her warm, little shack. Myra pulled out a pair of holey gloves from her coat pocket and put them on.

"We might be able to find an empty house to sleep in, but I find it all still a bit creepy to sleep in a house full of skeletons." Evy nodded in agreement. The idea was a bit unnerving to even think about.

"Let's go before it gets dark on us." Bagby strode behind them dragging the squeaky wagon.

"Oh, hush," Myra scolded him, as he whinnied in protest at the hideous noise.

The pointed, bony branches of the trees twisted skyward around them. They walked steadily in silence. The quietness of the woods around them reminded Myra how alone she had been for so long. It sent shivers down her back, and she unconsciously moved closer to Evy. Evy was lost in thought. She was trying not to be discouraged by her new surroundings.

Her mom always found the good in everything; she wished she was here now. Sometimes her uplifting statements would be so far of a reach that it would send both of them into rolling hysterical laughter.

When they reached the river, Evy's old comfort, the giant old oak tree, stood grandly by the now poisoned, green river. It was sick, but alive. It was the only tree that was not visibly rotting. The river itself was as still as death. Evy ran and wrapped her arms around the lovely oak tree. She wiped the tears from her eyes on her sleeve.

Her eyes traveled over the sickly river. There were no bugs, fish or snakes, in its green glassy depths, just death. The water tumbled heavily, thick with poison over the rocks. Only birds sung in the trees somewhere far away. They survived, because they could fly great distances to find clean water.

"Come on, we need to get moving. It will be dark before we know it," Myra urged, prying Evy's arms off of the giant tree. They walked beside the river towards town. They were careful not to get too close to the water.

They walked through the empty woods for hours in silence, following the green river's twisting path. They crossed over railroad tracks, silent and rusty, and left the company of the river of death. Beside the tracks, houses stood eerily hollow, staring out at them with blackened, broken windows.

The sun was starting to set, and they began to look for shelter. An old barn next to a farmhouse looked promising, so they headed for it. They all huddled inside for comfort from the whistling winter wind. Myra built a fire on the dirt floor of the barn. But, Evy immediately wished Myra had not. The light of the fire exposed the bones of dead horses lying forever bridled in their stalls. Their empty sunken eyes glared into Evy's very soul.

A terrible shudder rocked Evy's body. She was unsure if she would be able to sleep here at all. Myra seemed unnerved, but began to warm a can of green beans and some breaded eggplant up on the fire. The combination of horse bones, Clarence's awful stench and fried eggplant, made Evy queasy. She waved her dinner away.

Evy walked to the wagon and grabbed her quilt. She found a corner as far from the horse stalls as possible, laid her quilt down and tried her best to go to sleep. The thin walls of the barn shook from the thunderous, chilly wind outside and they kept Evy awake. She lay staring at Myra across the fire far away. Myra ate her eggplant and green beans in silence.

Evy studied Myra's youthful-looking face. She wondered, how old she was and how many secrets Myra must know? She wondered, how many Myra would tell her? She wondered how she could eat with the dead horses all around them. Evy's thoughts drifted her to sleep finally, but morning came all too quickly.

Their tired little band packed up and began moving again very early, right after a small breakfast of strange smelling orange-berry pie. Evy ate a few bites, but the horse bones still haunted her, and she could not finish her breakfast. Clarence finished off Evy's piece, and licked his fingers from on top of the wagon as they walked along.

They walked all day, passing house after house, row after row of death. As they came to the center of town, the golden rays of sunshine began to dip behind the hills. Small buildings and her old school house were visible through the sea of broken homes. Evy was glad to see something familiar not etched with the shadowy lines of unhappiness.

"Can we sleep in Ms. Eldran's classroom tonight? It would be nice to have some familiarity," Evy asked, hopefully.

Myra nodded, remembering Evy's aversion to the horse barn. "There won't be any bones in there, so it's a good spot. He only struck at night, so most people were at home."

Myra looked worried suddenly. She looked around her at the cluttered landscape in the fading light. "I think we are being watched," she whispered. "Keep alert." Their feet suddenly crunched too loudly on the broken, concrete parking lot of the school. Bagby's squeaky wagon wheels echoed painfully against the silent evening. But as they drew nearer, there was a deafening thunderous waterfall sound coming from behind the school. Evy hoped it would drown out their clatter.

A light flickered in one of the school windows, a small candle flame. Myra looked panicked. "Someone's already here. We need to move on."

"Okay. Let's go," Evy whispered. They all four turned back towards the town, but a man was standing in their way behind them. He was holding a rifle pointed in their direction.

The rifleman's mouth was clearly growling. He had a large, brown cowboy hat on top of his head. His stocky body could have pushed over a horse, and he wore a dark green shirt with the letters TPWD embroidered on it. Another man walked up and stood beside him carrying a broom with a sharpened handle. Around them, others began to circle, each one with a different weapon. Clarence freaked out and let go an awful stench, but it did not deter the henchmen. One man tried to hit Clarence with a bat, so he jumped off the wagon, and ran to his old home under the school. "He'll be fine there," Myra said, winking at Evy who seemed worried.

"Who are you?" The man with the rifle asked. "Are you with the Snake Pirates? Do you work for the King?"

Evy shook her head wildly. "No, we just needed a place to sleep."

"Evy? Is that you? I recognize your voice…but, it can't be." A lady wearing a long blue dress stepped through the circle of people. Her hair was dark and pulled into a bun, but it was her face that made Evy cry. It was her mom! Evy ran and threw her arms around her. Kyla began crying, too. She held her tightly in her arms for a really long time. When she let go, she studied her face long and hard. "How did Myra find you? I thought you were gone forever. You look the same. (Kyla scrunched her face up) Why haven't you changed in all these years?"

"Lady K, we should get in before the Snake Pirates come out to play," said the man with the rifle.

"Yes, yes. We should. Come on in. I want to hear everything."

They were led inside the school. The man with the rifle followed closely, and it was clear by the looks he was giving that he did not trust them. Inside, there were people of all ages and colors. There were at least fifty men, women and children, clean and healthy. They seemed to have found a way to survive graciously. The crowd moved respectfully out of Evy's mom's way as she walked, as if she were royalty. The thundering sound echoed loudly around them. It sounded like a torrential rain storm outside, but it was a cloudless, sapphire-blue night.

Evy's mom walked to a podium and addressed the curious crowd. They grew silent and only the echoing thunder could be heard. "My fellow refugees, I would like to present to you, my daughter, Evy. This is my Aunt Myra as well. It is such a miracle to have them here with me. I thought my daughter was lost forever. She and Myra, like me, are Lippoliks. Their powers can help us all. Please welcome them as you would any peace-loving refugee. Charlie, (she gestured to the rifle man) please tell Roberta to prepare a feast for our guests." The crowd began to whisper among each other. Then, they began to chant,

"Welcome and long live the Lippoliks! Long live Lady K!" She stepped down, and rushed back to Evy. They walked hand in hand towards the back door. Myra and Bagby headed outside, too.

"I have something to show you," Kyla said smiling hugely.

They stepped outside into the crisp, night air. The thunder they had heard earlier was louder now. They headed toward Evy's old cafeteria. Flashes of lighting could be seen through the windows in the doors of the old building. Kyla unlocked a large padlock and pushed open the doors. Inside, there was a miniature storm. Rain fell in sheets on budding plants in pots on the concrete floor. Large fruit trees, tomatoes, green beans, oranges and more were growing brilliantly from the small storm's nourishment.

"I found great need here of my power here, and I have learned to control it well, too. The water that falls from my storms is collected in buckets and it is fresh. No snake pirate can poison it, because I can always produce more from the sky. We check it three random times a day for contaminants. It also waters the plants twice a day, so that we have food to eat. Pretty clever, huh?"

Evy looked around in awe. Her mother had become the hero that she had always known she could be. She had no words to describe her pride, and so, she just hugged her mom tightly.

"I missed you so much!" Evy's tears began to fall, blending with the soft rain. She felt the tingles of her trigger play to her emotion down her back, but she ignored it. She also ignored the red feathers that popped out of the top of her head.

"Dinner time!" someone yelled to them, from the back door of the school.

"Yay!" Myra squeaked and walked quickly out of the door. Evy had forgotten Myra was there.

Inside, they had turned the old library tables into dining tables. Books still lined the dusty shelves around them. "We use this room for everything. It is our breakfast room in the morning, our school room during the day, our lunch room, and our dinner room." Kyla laughed. "We love this room. The classrooms have become homes now. There are about two families to each classroom. Since there are four in here and three side trailers, we have approximately fourteen families living here with us. Occasionally, a drifter will come through. We have room for more in the gym, but there aren't that many survivors out there." Her face dropped suddenly, burdened with pain. Evy noticed the weary wrinkles lining her sweet eyes. Those were new.

A thin, middle-aged woman with long, blonde hair walked slowly over to Evy. A small, golden child clung to her hip; his beautiful yellow ringlets fell softly on his angelic face. He was sucking on his tiny thumb. The lady smiled kindly and stood waiting for an invitation to sit down.

"Please, sit down, Adeline," Kyla said. Evy stood at the mention of her name.

"Adeline, it is so good to see that you made it!" She walked around the table and hugged her old friend tightly. The baby squealed with joy.

Myra was at the doorway fighting with Charlie, the rifle man, about Bagby coming to eat with them in the dining room. Her hair was all static and swirling in circles around her head. Her arms were flailing wildly, but she, despite her outrageous appearance, was apparently losing the fight. Bagby turned and went out the back door in search of some sweet grass or tree bark, not his first choice for a meal, but it would do. Myra could not tell them that he used to be human and Kyla did not tell them what Myra's powers were, either, for fear of panicking the people.

A rotund black lady, with a gray balding head, entered the room carrying trays of sumptuous food. There were roasted carrots and potatoes with gravy. There were about five different kinds of vegetables, too, in large pots: peas, carrots, cabbage, lima beans and sweet potatoes. Warm cornbread was brought out on skillets and filled the air with a rich aroma. Then for their dessert, a large shiny platter piled high with delectable fruit. Clear, fresh water in shining goblets was passed around the room and toasts were made to God, providence, Lady K and the newcomers. Evy's mouth was watering in anticipation. She had not eaten in awhile.

The room became filled with merriment, as everyone filled their plates and started eating. The sounds of metal forks clinking on china filled the room. Everyone seemed so completely happy that it was hard to imagine the horror that waited for them outside the walls of the school, or the sadness that overshadowed America.

After dinner, Kyla, Myra and Evy watched the children play in the fenced playground in the setting sun. Their merriment was contagious. It was a welcome gift. Evy and Kyla talked breathlessly, trying to catch each other up. Tears tumbled down Kyla's face as she talked about her boys. The story was the same as Myra's and just as filled with sadness, but for one difference.

Bowen had gone missing along with Big Papa. Kyla had gone to look for him two years ago at Big Papa's farm. She was going to rally the family against Kallon and try to stop the madness he was creating. When she arrived at the farm, however, she found it torn apart and no one was there. The house had been burned down. So, she returned home, hoping to see if Bowen might be there.

She had found her own home burned to the ground as well. Kyla knew Kallon was behind it. He was looking for something. Family members were disappearing all around her one by one, as she sought them out. Kyla thought perhaps he was kidnapping them. She did not know for sure. Myra sat quietly listening beside them. The fear of Evy's brother was in her mom's eyes as well.

When it became too dark to see, they rose and headed back to the school with everyone else. Watchmen were posted at the doors to the school. Two body guards walked Myra, Bagby, Kyla and Evy by candlelight to her mom's quarters, Ms. Eldran's old room.

"I chose this room, because it still has some of your artwork hanging on the wall. It was nice to have a piece of you near me."

The two bodyguards stayed by the door, and Myra stuck out her tongue at them as she hauled in Bagby. All the desks had been removed and there were four twin beds in the room. The wagon and water jugs had been brought inside earlier. The room was large enough to accommodate Bagby, also. He went and curled up in the corner.

Evy went and washed her face in a basin sitting on a desk. She took off her boots and socks. She put her lovely, ruby bracelet inside of one of her boots. Then she braided her long, red hair.

By the time she was finished Myra was snoring loudly in one of the beds. Her mom was sitting in the other one watching her in the candlelight. "I've missed you so much." She said softly.

Evy smiled, "I just saw you yesterday." Her mom laughed and they both crawled into the same bed, not wanting to leave each other's side. Evy fell asleep with a smile still on her face and her mom's arms wrapped tightly around her.

CHAPTER 9:
THE MIDNIGHT FIGHT

A loud crash startled Evy awake. There was shouting and screaming coming from outside the door. It was still dark outside, but there was a strange glow shining from the window. She looked to her side to find that her mom was not in the bed. Myra was snoring loudly still, despite the loud noises outside, and Bagby was standing by the classroom door whining. He whinnied loudly at Evy and kicked at the door. Evy stuffed her feet into her boots and hurried to the door. As soon as she opened it, Bagby burst rudely out of it ahead of her.

Only one guard was standing by her door, and she wondered where her mom was. Her eyes caught sight of a fire glowing brightly as it chewed its way through the cafeteria. She ran in that direction. The scene that unfolded before her was like a terrible nightmare. There was chaos everywhere.

There were men wearing green masks attacking the refugees. They must have set the life-giving cafeteria on fire, and the doors and windows of the school were busted in. The attackers and the refugees were using the broken boards from the school doors to fight with. Gunfire and loud screams filled the air, which was overshadowed by a large storm that was electrifying various masked men. Thunder crashed loudly and bolts of lighting zipped hotly through the dark, night sky blending with the glow of the ravenous fire.

Evy looked up towards the roof and found her mom standing on top of it like a grand conductor. Her arms were above her head and her black hair was flying wildly around her infuriated face. Charlie stood beside her, his rifle pointed and ready. Evy was so afraid. She looked around her, unsure of what to do.

In the bright flashes of lightning, she caught glimpses of something she was just noticing. There were dozens of animals in the fight also: pigs, sheep, a horse, a kangaroo and smaller animals, too. They were clawing biting and kicking at the refugees. The sound they were making was like being at the zoo at lunchtime. They were all yelling in their animal voices. And most interesting of all was that all of their butts were purple. A man in a green mask ran screaming past her with Clarence attached to his face with his claws. Clarence waved when he saw her and then commenced his scratching. Dr. Bagby and a black horse wearing lipstick were kicking at each other furiously.

Evy's fear was changing her. With the image of the animals in her mind, she decided to fight instead of disappear, so she was triggering. Her body sprouted red feathers and she began to twist and morph. Her feet became paws and her hands twisted into large, three-toed talons. Wings painfully sprouted from her shoulder blades, until a large, red griffin stood in her place. It was the first time she was able to control what she had become. Her red feathers glistened in the glow of lightning and fire. The back of her body blended into the golden fur of a lion. It was the creature she had avoided becoming all this time. She felt free. She raised her wings and tried to fly. It was easier than she thought. She lifted lightly off the ground and hovered over everyone's heads.

A few green, masked men looked up at her and panicked, running into the woods. She flew up to the roof and landed clumsily. Her mom looked at her and saw Evy in the creature's eyes. She tried to speak to her mom, but it just came out as loud, high-pitched squawks. Kyla looked at her knowingly.

"It'll be okay. We can win this tonight." Two ducks flew up after her.

"Where is Myra?" They quacked loudly. But Myra was nowhere in sight still. Evy was shocked that she could hear them speak though. She reasoned it was probably because she was an animal herself.

The ducks were no match for her, however. She was much larger. She had talons and claws on her side. They had flippers, so they flew away within moments. The other animals below, too, were chanting for Myra. She could not let them find her, or they would tear her apart.

Getting braver now, she dove off the roof, knocking a green mask off his feet and onto his back in the grass. Another one swung a large board at her and she caught it in her talons. Then she lifted him off his feet and carried him through the air as he screamed like a girl. She dropped him in the top of a tree, where he clung tightly and continued screaming. When she landed back on the ground, she felt something chewing at her ankle. An evil-looking possum was biting her. She recognized him for a moment, as the possum in the hole from long ago, and then kicked him sharply in the teeth. Three masks jumped on her at once, because she now posed the largest threat. One of them plucked a red feather from her wing. She squawked and spread her large wings, knocking two of them to the ground. She kicked and scratched and they ran bruised and bloody from her. Not one stood against her now. She chased them into the woods and went back for more. Lighting zipped around her, precisely zapping her enemies. Then she would finish them off, intimidating and chasing them into the woods.

Some of them were braver, and she would have to carry them to the edge of the woods before they would lose their nerve and run away. She worked continuously. Only a few were still fighting by the time she was through. The few that were left were chased off by the entire group of refugees, who were shouting and waving sticks, shovels and bats in the air.

The refugees all stood there a moment staring into the empty woods, reassuring themselves that the Snake Pirates would not come back. A rainstorm was already putting out the fire in the cafeteria, but they would not be able to see how bad the damage was until morning.

The wounded were carried into the gym on Bagby's back and laid on blankets and towels. It looked like everyone had survived and only a few were badly hurt.

Evy's feathers molted from her body, and she began to take her human form once again. Her mom climbed down from the roof by way of a ladder leaned against the wall. Everything was getting much calmer. "Are you okay?" Her mom asked.

"Yeah, you?"

"Fine. That was amazing what you did! That griffin you turned into was pretty awesome! You scared the mess out of those Snake Pirates." Her mom looked at her with pride; her hair was piled on her head in a disheveled mess.

"Thanks, you were pretty awesome yourself," Evy added, "With the whole, 'I eat lightning for breakfast' look going on. You were just zapping bad guys left and right."

"Yeah, well, I've had practice."

They walked together to the gym to check on the wounded. The injuries they saw could all be fixed by Myra's magic, so Evy decided to go and find her. She left the gym and headed back toward her room, taking the path down the sidewalk in the light of the glowing moon.

As she drew closer, she saw the guard lying on the ground outside of her door. When she got next to him, she knew he was dead. He had a pained look on his pale greenish face. His body was curled up like a discarded napkin. She knelt down and touched his icy cold skin. He was definitely dead.

The door to the class was open a crack. Evy's heart beat hard in her chest, and she felt herself triggering. This time she chose invisibility. She waved and faded into thin air. Cautiously, she made her way up the steps. She pushed the door open slowly and stepped inside.

Myra was sitting on her bed tied up with ropes. She was gagged, too. Her blue eyes were wide with fear and her hair was flying with static above her head. There was someone standing over her whispering in her ear. He was wearing a black, hooded, leather jacket, and he held a sparkling dagger in his left hand shaped like a wavy snake.

She prayed she was as invisible as she hoped she was. Evy crept closer, hoping to hear what he was saying to Myra and unsure of what to do. Her legs felt wobbly and her knees were giving out on her. Her fear was taking over her mind. She tripped on air and fell with a thud.

The man in black turned around quickly, and Evy screamed. It was the person she feared the most. It was John! John was alive, and he was standing in the same room with her. She sat paralyzed with terror on the floor.

John searched the room with his evil, black eyes for the source of the scream he heard, but could not find anyone. He waved the dagger in the empty air maliciously over Evy's head and then bolted from the room. Myra sat stoically on her bed. Her eyes fixed on the door.

Evy waited a few minutes and then calmed herself down enough to become visible once again. Her body rippled back to reality. She rushed to Myra and began untying her. "Are you okay?" she asked.

Myra frowned and shook her head, no. Evy helped her to her feet. "What happened?" She asked.

"Ya'll leave me in here to die all alone, that's what happened. And I thought I had put the fear in that boy years ago, but he came after me in my sleep. I was too afraid to be annoyed and could not do anything about it."

"What was John doing here?" Evy asked, still terrified. To her surprise, Myra laughed.

"That wasn't John, dear. John's dead. That was Kallon. He can make you hallucinate. You see him as the thing you are most afraid of. It's one of his triggers. He has a few. The strangest one is his stretchy arms. They're like gum. I think he was looking for something or someone. He kept asking me where the bird girl was. I figured he must have meant you. He must want to find you really badly, or he would not have come himself."

"Oh," was all Evy could muster as a response. "Well, we may have left you in here to die, but it was only because we were fighting a war outside with the Snake Pirates."

"Oh," Myra whispered back.

"We could use your help with the wounded. Can you whip up some healing potion for them real quick? I saw the supplies in your bag."

"I'll get them. I don't want you nosing around in there, messing with my stuff."

She got off the bed and mixed up some potion, then zapped it with her purple-lightning, pinky finger. She did not bother putting pants on; she just marched out the door in her bloomers and a short night shirt. Evy followed on her heels.

When they got to the gym, Myra set about healing the injured people. Evy headed over to her mom to tell her about her run in with Kallon. Her mom listened intently. Then she called two men over and told them to go and collect the dead guard from outside Evy's room. She did not want anyone else knowing about him yet, until his cause of death was determined.

The orange rays of the morning sun were glowing in the horizon by the time they had finished tending to the injuries. Myra's potion worked faster on some than it did on others. Some people took two or even three coats before they began to feel better.

Evy wondered if they would be upset that they would be stained purple on the places where the medicine was applied. Because of that small side effect, Myra had refused to put any on wounds received on their faces. People were only grateful short term and they almost always complained later when the need for healing was gone.

"The scars are better than the stain because the scars aren't my fault," Myra explained. There were two people, however, for whom it could not be helped. Their head injuries would have killed them without the potion, so it was applied despite the staining side effects. One of them was a small girl, about ten, who had been hit in the side of the head with a plank. Her hair turned purple the instance the potion touched it.

"Boy, Myra you really do leave your mark on the world don't you?" Evy said, "Literally." Myra did not think that she was clever at all and gave her a dirty look.

When they finished, they headed back to bed to try and catch a few hours of weary sleep. After locking the door tightly, they fell heavily on their beds and straight asleep. Evy's mom was still tending to business inside the school, however.

It was nearly one o'clock in the afternoon when Evy awoke. She made her way dazed, into the school building, her eyes thick with sleep crusts. Lunch was being cleaned from the Library tables. She followed the servers back to the kitchen in hopes that there might be a few leftovers for her. The gray haired cook looked her over with contempt at her lateness, but gave her a heaping plate of food to eat anyway. Everyone she passed in the hallway stared at her and whispered, "That's the girl who turned into a griffin." A few smaller kids wanted her autograph, including the little girl with the purple hair.

She headed outside to see the cafeteria's damage in the daylight. Her mom stood directing repairs in the yard to a few able-bodied men. Half of the building was burned to cinders, along with half their crops. Evy put one arm around her mom's shoulders. Kyla kissed her forehead. Her eyes were red and had dark circles around them. She had not slept at all. "You should go get some sleep, Mom. They can handle it from here."

"They haven't slept, either. It would not be fair of me, as their leader. Besides, if we don't finish, then we don't eat. When you finish your food, though, I need to show you something."

Evy understood. She sat on a swing on the playground to eat her lunch and watch. Bagby limped over to her and sniffed her plate, so she fed him a corn muffin. He nibbled it contently glad to have human food in his mouth for the first time in days. Myra tromped out of the school door bearing a large plate of food also. Evy was glad that she was dressed and washed. Her blonde hair was pulled back into a neat bun. Evy hoped that Clarence was okay, she had not seen him since the fight last night.

They ate together in silence. When they had finished, Evy walked back to her mom. Myra followed. Kyla led them back to the school, up the stairway and into the attic. It was dark and musky. A few candles provided the only light in the room. There were shelves with medical equipment on them and some storage boxes for the refugees piled in one corner. The dead, green guard lay on a table in the middle of the room. Charlie stood over him.

"Charlie has determined his cause of death as poison. The tests were positive for the presence of the same poison that is found in the water of the rivers and lakes, but in a highly concentrated dose. The guard didn't even see it coming. We tested our water supply, too and it was negative, so the Snake Pirates must not have gotten to it last night. We have concluded, as expected, that Kallon must have killed him to gain entrance to your room last night. It's the first person he's ever killed of my refugees. He usually leaves me in peace. We've drawn our lines in the sand. Something must have provoked him to this. He's out of control."

Myra shook her head sadly and clucked her tongue. "We need to do something, or he'll wipe us all out."

"I thought of something already. I can't go with you though, I'm needed here. Myra, you have to go find Jack. He's our only hope. He's the most powerful of all of us Lippoliks. He is the only one who can save us. Find Jack, and then, Myra, please find Bowen. Maybe Jack knows where Kallon is hiding him and Big Papa."

"Who's Jack?" Evy asked.

Myra shook her head, ignoring Evy's question. "I won't go alone. He's dangerous. I'm not even sure I can find him."

"I can't go with you. These people need me here."

Evy waved her hand in the air. "Hello! I can go. I made it here, didn't I? I fought off dozens of Snake Pirates last night...as a griffin. I think I can handle finding this Jack person. Besides, I put all of you in danger by being here. Myra said he's looking for a griffin or bird creature or whatever...that's me."

Her mom looked at her miserably. "But I just got you back. How did he even know you were a griffin? I can't let you leave again so soon. I can't lose you again."

"I'm glad to see you, too, but you can't leave and Myra won't go alone, so there's no other option. I'll be fine, and I promise to come back sooner this time." She smiled reassuringly at her.

"I don't know... I guess that I have enough work to keep me occupied till you return. Stay close to Myra, and take Fluffy with you, in case you need to send for me to come and help you, or once you have found Jack. Fluffy is much faster and smarter than a normal pigeon. I'll find you." She gestured towards a blue pigeon cooing in a cage.

"You should leave as soon as possible, I suppose, tomorrow morning at the latest. Keep your bracelet on you at all times, because I have found that it will ward you from other Lippolik power. My earrings have saved me and others, a few times already from Kallon. I discovered the jewelry's power to keep me safe when Kallon first turned thirteen. I used them to save Bowen once, too. It will keep you safe from Kallon, Jack and …Myra." She gave Myra a slight mocking smile. Myra rolled her eyes and stuck out her tongue.

Evy looked down at her beautiful bracelet. She had put it back on this morning, but wished she had put it on last night now, because of her run in with Kallon. She admired it once again with new eyes, knowing now that it protected her. "I think that Kallon is after you and Myra, for what ever reason. Once you leave, I think they will leave us alone for awhile. Myra, I trust you to keep her safe. If anything happens to her…" Her eyes said the rest.

They headed downstairs again. They had much to prepare. Evy was sad about leaving her mom again, but she was determined to fix the damage her half-brother had caused. Myra would need help, too. She would not do much without her. She always needed a push.

Myra and Kyla went back to Mrs. Eldran's classroom to pour over maps and try to locate possible places Jack could be. They were there arguing for at least an hour. They finally came to a reasonable agreement on his possible location, though, a few towns away. Evy went outside to relax before dinner. She looked at the bracelet a moment, puzzling over it and admiring its intricate design. Then she put the bracelet back on her wrist, and sat on the swings. Her legs kicked off the ground. She swung higher and higher, upwards through the icy air. Her mind drifted back to when she was flying as a griffin. She felt so free when she was in the air and lucky to have such an exciting and powerful trigger. She stretched her arms to the sky and closed her eyes as the wind ruffled through her hair. The dinner bell rang. Evy counted to three and jumped out of the swing, flying through the air. She raced inside famished.

Dinner was wonderfully delicious and oddly enough, a little blackened. It was hard to enjoy it, though, while her mother was crying across the table, staring at her while she was eating. It made her cry as well, but she kept eating, choking her food down. Myra had opted to eat her food outside with Bagby to escape the emotions inside.

Despite the melancholy atmosphere, though, Evy was excited to be doing something constructive that might lead to happiness for everyone once again. She did not feel right just sitting around while the world died.

That night, she fell asleep heavily, the rain on the roof drumming softly and soothing. Her mom, of course, was the reason for it. Kyla tossed and turned, crying quietly to herself and praying for her daughter's well being. Myra's hearty snores were throbbing in Kyla's head, too.

Evy woke to birds singing the next morning. Her mom's bed was empty, yet again. She headed to breakfast, and found her mother ashen-faced and sitting alone at the main table. Kyla smiled weakly at Evy. It was a gesture that pained Evy more than cheered her.

After breakfast was cleared away, everyone headed outside like a huge flock of birds. It was time for them to go. Bagby was already hitched to the wagon again and the wheels were thoughtfully greased this time, much to his delight.

Evy and her mother held each other at long length, but Myra just sighed and kept her distance from all the well-wishing. The people were adamant about letting her know how important this mission was to them. Evy assured them that she would do her best to find Jack and end their suffering. With long waves of goodbye, they were off. Clarence was hopping and flipping for the crowd's enjoyment from atop Bagby's back. A slight drizzling rain fell on them as they headed down the road. Evy knew it was because of her mom's crying, but she did not let herself turn around for fear she might change her mind and stay.

CHAPTER 10:

A HERO AMONG US

It was a glorious morning to be traveling. The sun shone brightly above, but it still rained far away in the distance behind them. It was a beautiful day to be alive despite the death all around them. The landscape was a much different picture during the day than at night. There was silence everywhere. Empty rotting houses and broken trees lined weedy, cracked streets. There were no dogs barking or bees buzzing, just infinite, deafening silence.

Rusty cars sat parked in driveways and streets. Their would-be passengers lay still inside, skinless in the bathtub. Evy wished that she could ride in those cars, but all of their gasoline had been siphoned out long ago by survivors for running lots of different things, like generators. She thought of the ones who had not survived. Every house that they passed was holding a bone family inside, dried and silent. As they walked along, Evy's tears began to fall, one for each home destroyed by her half-brother. A river of tears flowed for all the silence that surrounded her.

Dr. Bagby still limped from last night's fight with the pirates and his tail smelled like burnt toast. Myra did not believe in healing minor injuries. She believed that the body needed to fight some things on its own, unless it was her, of course. Evy was glad that everyone had survived.

Myra whistled and swayed to the song "Oklahoma," stopping every once in a while to shout "Oklahoma!" at the top of her lungs. She was happy to be alone again. She was obviously not a people person. She even wore a bright pink shirt with sunflowers on it to reflect her mood. She also wore many necklaces around her neck with every kind of good luck charm imaginable hanging from them: rabbit's foot, four leaf clovers, garlic, blue beads and crosses. It was a superstitious overload.

Her happy spirit was starting to get on Evy's nerve, though, who was trying to forget the horrific parts of last night's fight and the death that encompassed them. The more she sang, the madder Evy became.

"How can you be so cheerful? Oh, I know...perhaps, because last night you slept through the whole fight!" Evy shouted sarcastically. "We could have died and all you did was snore away, as if nothing was happening."

"I had a great dream, too," Myra replied, smiling happily. "Earplugs sometimes are the perfect solution to a stressful day. Besides, you handled the situation well enough without me. You handled the Kallon situation easily, too. I heard it was an awesome sight; you carrying bad guys over the tree tops and hurling them through the air. All while, triggered as a red-feathered griffin. I'm sorry, I missed it."

Just then, they rounded the corner. A murky creek ran along a rocky path and a small bridge hung over it so low, it looked as if it was dipping its toes in the cool water to escape the heat of the day. Evy wished she could lay in it and roll in its chilly ripples. It was always hot in the afternoon, even in the winter. The cold morning was already gone, and the afternoon felt like a blanket that was wrapped too tightly around her.

On the other side of the bridge, two hills rose high together littered with brush, cacti and a few dead trees. Bagby stood between the hills waiting and licking his wounds. He had kept a pretty strong lead in front of them the whole time. Myra stepped slowly and cautiously onto the swinging bridge. The longing to swim was in her eyes same as Evy's. It had been such a very long time since she had even had a bath. There was never water to spare for such activities. Evy followed close behind. When they reached the other side, Evy helped Myra gather cactus for some of her medicinal purposes.

Suddenly, a twig snapped and Bagby's ears stood at attention. Five smutty Snake Pirates walked around one hill and stood in their path. The largest man stepped forward, obviously in charge. He was carrying a large piece of wood, which was probably a piece of the school from last night's fight. He waved it in their direction menacingly.

"I remember you," he spat out between his yellowed, crooked teeth. The others laughed behind him. "You're all alone against the five of us today, griffin girl. Tell your friend there that she can wait on the side, because we're gonna rough you up. We got no quarrel with her." His minions laughed again.

"How dare you!" Myra looked shocked, but could not help but smile; her happy mood was just that good.

He ignored her self-righteous proclamation and continued. "So, we'll be taking that beast of burden with us now. Just think of it as taxes to your blessed King

Kallon," he sneered, pointing at Bagby with his plank of wood.

Myra leaned over to whisper to Evy, "Twist my ear."

"What?" Evy looked confused.

"Twist my ear, girl. I'm in too good a mood right now to be annoyed and…"

"What?" Evy asked again. She was preoccupied with weighing her options against five grown men. She could only turn into a little griffin, which was much too small to take on five men.

"Never mind!" And with that, the air became even hotter. The Snake Pirates began to look a bit scared and confused; they had not counted on her having powers also. Their hair stood straight up in the air. Electrical static pulsed heavily in the air around them. Myra's eyes were squeezed shut and her lips pursed. She pointed her stubby fingers at the pirates and then Zap, Crack, Boom!

Three white sheep stood bleating pathetically in front of them looking totally confused. Their wool had white smoke rising off of it. The remaining two pirates had turned tail and run away after seeing their sheepy comrades.

"I'll be keeping Bagby with me," she said. Then she kicked the largest sheep in the ribs. He bit her leg in retaliation and Myra zapped him again. His back leg started twitching rather badly. He tried to walk, but fell on his side every few feet.

"Well, that would have come in handy last night!" Evy's eyes looked as if on fire.

"I can only change three at a time, for some weird reason. It usually drains all my power for the rest of the day. Two got away. I suppose they'll go and tell the King what I did, so much for a quiet, peaceful journey. Anyway, it wouldn't have done any good against an army of those guys like last night. I guess I could have zapped them with my electrical bursts, but truthfully it would have only annoyed them." Myra looked truly apologetic and began to rummage in her rainbow bag. "Ah, sheep sheers. We can sell the wool in town for a home-cooked meal. It's too hot for wool today anyway."

Evy decided to forgive Myra. She grabbed the twitching leader sheep by the neck so Myra could sheer him. Dr. Bagby was relieved to still be with them and had been pleasantly surprised that Myra cared. He held one sheep down with his front hoof to be helpful.

Their bags were stuffed full of wool (two bags from the largest sheep) so the set off for town. There was no room for the packs of wool on wagon, so Myra and Evy carried them. It was a hard walk. They had to avoid the main road, because the King would be watching them. He had spies posted all along the main roads. The wool was heavy and hot. Sweat trickled down Evy's back, and she wished to swim once again. Buildings began to appear on the horizon and they got bigger the more they walked. Neither of them was talking much anymore, mostly because of all of their burdensome loads. Evy began to dream of a lovely spread of supper like the one she had enjoyed at breakfast. She closed her eyes and tasted the goodness in her mind.

The buildings were in view now and it was heartbreaking to see them freshly burned. The Snake Pirates must have stopped here first yesterday. Myra's face looked taut and angry.

"I knew some of these people well. They were good folks. I had heard there were only twenty or so still here that were able to survive and make drinkable water. They had refused to leave their town. I came here with Bagby once a year to get supplies and a warm meal before the dead water. I knew them all very well. How could he do this? How can he just kill good, innocent people?" Evy just shook her head. She sat down on the dirt. Tears were welling in her eyes.

"I don't understand how someone gets this hateful. How someone with such love around them can choose to hate? I feel so sad." Myra looked confused, because she was actually getting emotional. She quickly smashed the feeling deep down inside and wiped her nose on her sleeve.

"We should probably keep going, then," Evy whispered. "After we look for survivors, I mean."

Evy lifted herself off the ground and headed for the nearest building, a church. She left her wool pack behind. Myra went in the opposite direction, calling names out as she went.

The church was smoky and dusty inside. There were pieces of crusty, black ceiling littering the ground. A stain-glassed window washed the floor in soft, colored light. Evy listened intently. Silence. There was silence everywhere she went lately. It was a heavy deafening silence. There was so much silence that her feet crunching on the burnt floorboards was actually calming, because it was something to hear. There were no people in any of the rooms, so she returned to the Bagby and Clarence.

They shook their heads, no. They hadn't found anyone either. Myra took the longest to come back. She drug her feet heavily through the dirt when she finally returned. "Maybe they've escaped, or they will go stay with my mom," Evy said hopefully.

Myra looked up at them wearily, burdened with sadness, and loaded her wool pack back on her back. Clarence climbed back on the wagon and the four of them headed towards the shelter of the lifeless trees in the distance.

A winter chill was beginning to blow again as evening settled. It made the wool on Evy's back become less burdensome suddenly, because it warmed her. As darkness began to descend, however, Evy's stomach was growling loudly. The noise was so loud that Clarence broke into a fit of giggles every time it rumbled.

Myra found a good, soft, sandy spot under a short cliff beside a creek and began to set up camp. Evy helped her unload and set up the tent. After the tent was set up, Myra took great care to draw a perfect circle around it to ward off evil spirits. Bagby found a soft scarce patch of grass to nibble, and Clarence went in search of some small sticks to start a fire.

When the fire was finally glowing and swaying in the growing wind, they popped open some canned beans from their wagon. Evy un-wrapped a package of cornbread her mother had packed them. Myra had brought some fresh melon, too, from her garden. They warmed the cans of beans in the fire and passed one to everyone. Bagby's had to be dumped on a flat rock, so he could lick it up, but everyone else used a spoon. It was definitely not the best meal ever, but Evy's stomach quit talking to her. The fire crackled and spit warmly. Clarence was already sound asleep. His little paws dripping with bean juice and his face covered in it as well. Myra stirred the fire and sighed heavily. Her mind was elsewhere. Evy watched her keenly. She had no idea where they were headed to, or what. She wanted to prepare herself.

The wind was picking up. It stirred the fire menacingly, threatening to extinguish its warmth. The air was easier to breathe in the wind, though. It must have traveled from far away to be so thick with oxygen. Evy closed her eyes and took a deep, glorious breathe. Her chest loosened a bit. Her heart's sadness and stress was lifted a little.

"So, who is Jack?" she asked, feeling suddenly refreshed.

Myra did not look up, but she stopped stirring the fire. "He's my youngest brother, your uncle."

"And…" Evy pressed.

"And…he is very powerful and hard to find. He is a hermit, much like me. I haven't seen him in a very long time. I'm not that sure that we can find him. Last I heard he was living in a swamp somewhere up in a tree, or something."

"Oh. So, what are his triggers?" Myra did not answer right away. She seemed content to sit in silence.

"Well? I would like to know what I'm headed to. Don't I deserve to know? Why does everything Lippolik have to be such a huge secret?"

"I don't know them all. He is very emotional, like you. His favorite trigger is teleportation, but he has many others."

"Well, that was…vague." It was unusual to get even that much information out of Myra, though, so Evy pressed her further. She wanted to take advantage of the situation.

"Can you tell me about my grandmother? I've never met her and Mom doesn't mention her often. You said she triggered like me? What was she like?"

"Is. What _is_ she like? She is still alive. She disappeared when Kyla was eleven, but she didn't die. She's around. She is looking for something. Once she finds it, she'll return. It's just taking her a while to find it, I guess." Evy could tell Myra missed her and was actually enjoying remembering her. The strong breeze was starting to stir up dust. Without grass to hold it down, it blew thickly around them. Myra dug into her rainbow bag and handed Evy a surgical mask, so it would be easier to breath. She put one on Bagby and Clarence, too.

To Evy's joyous surprise Myra continued talking. "She was a shape-shifter, but unlike you it was her only trigger. She could only shift into dog-like creatures: Chihuahua, hyena, werewolf or man's best friend. You know, things like that. It seems to me that you are an aviary-shifter. Birds only. It goes like that usually, only able to turn into one type of creature. Even when it was me turning you; you were a duck.

But, she got stuck one day. Couldn't shift back, so she left. It was all my fault. So, I took care of your mom till she went to college. But, she still missed her so much. We both did. I hope she finds it...Okay enough questions. You ask too many questions." She grew silent again, her face heavy with pain. Evy sat silent, too, but just for a moment.

"Where is your thirteenth birthday jewelry? I never see you wear any."

Myra glared at Evy, crossed her arms and closed her eyes. She was shut off from the world again, lost in her own mind's turmoil. No more questions would get through her shield of silence.

Evy could tell that that was all she was going to get tonight. She did not want to annoy her, that would be bad, and it was hard to hear her through the mask anyway. Her eyes were starting to burn from all the swirling sand, too. It was time for bed. She went and gathered up Clarence and carried him still snoring to the tent.

Bagby had cuddled closer into the side of the cliff to avoid the sandstorm. Myra opened one eye to make sure that Evy had finished interrogating her and then went inside the tent. She stepped carefully over her now mussed up circle and zipped up the tent tightly, but sand was already clouding the inside of the tent.

The fire outside was smothered as the sand buried it. Evy laid Clarence down at the end of her sleeping bag in the bed of wool Myra had made. She curled up and tried to sleep as the sandstorm outside began to rage and shake the sides of the tent.

A large, purple-butted owl blinked painfully at the sand stinging his glossy, luminous eyes. The owl had been sitting still as stone in a tree above the tent. His legs were stiff. He waited till he could hear Myra's muffled snoring and then flew away. He flew back to the comfort of the P.B.U. The owl was eager to share his valuable information with Rufus and Gus. Myra was going to go and find Jack, but who was Jack? "Who, who, who?" He repeated in the darkness to himself, as he battled his way home through the sandy wind.

CHAPTER 11:

NO-EARS

The sun rose, creeping over the tops of the trees and stretching their barren shadows over the tent top. Evy was warm in a tomb of sand. She smiled dreamily beneath her mask. Myra had already begun the morning chores. She dug Bagby out of the sand, because one of his legs had been buried rather deep. Then, she carried the large, heavy glass jars with their purple flowers to the river and ladled two spoonfuls of sludgy, green water into them. Next, she began to build a new fire pit, because the old one had been buried in the sand. They needed breakfast. Clarence meandered out of the tent scratching his purple butt. His fur was matted and the places where the beans had dripped were now clumps of hard mud that dangled like jewelry from it.

Evy stretched her arms, pushing the dirt as she did into little mountains. Her clothes and blankets were covered in it. When she sat up, a waterfall of sand cascaded down her body.

She could hear Myra whistling outside. The winter air bit her in the face rudely when she emerged from the tent, and she wished for her warm, sandy cocoon back. Her clothes felt itchy and she was pretty sure there was sand in her underwear. She went and sat on a rock by the green river. She watched as it tumbled like thick gelatin over the stones. A large, black tube sat still in the thick center of the river. The bones of a tuber lay on it, relaxing forever more, a soda in his bony hand.

Myra dug some more cornbread out of the wagon and some cactus apples from the day before. She mashed the apples up and added some sweet berries from her pack. She spread the homemade jam on the cornbread after she had warmed it on the fire. She gave some to Bagby, Clarence and some crumbs to Fluffy the pigeon still sleeping in his cage. Then she made her way over to Evy by the river. Myra looked comical with her sand-covered face. It was only sandy from the eyes up where her mask had not covered it and her blonde hair was hanging in dreads. Evy stifled her laugh though, because she was pretty sure she looked the same.

The sun began to climb and their little band of heroes headed out. Myra had decided to try, once again, to find life in the next town. She sat on the wagon atop all the mass of stuff and read the maps Kyla had drawn up. Bagby was straining and sweating heavily at the added load, but said nothing to Myra about it. He was a gentleman after all. Evy lived dreamily in her head and kept wandering off the path, where she would wake from her daydreams, panic and find her way back. This amused Clarence immensely as he watched from his perch on Bagby's back. They walked until sunset, and there was still no sign of a town. The sun was setting fast, so Myra decided to set up camp.

The swirls of sand were beginning their nightly torment. There was no time to build a fire, before it took them over. Consequently, they ate cold canned beets with some canned tuna, which Evy was very unsure of. The meal made her sick. Her legs hurt, too, from all the walking. She lay in the tent with her mask on barely breathing and for the first time was truly miserable. The darkness took over and the wind howled and beat at the walls of the tent. Far away, something else howled as well.

At first she thought she was hearing things. She had not heard a coyote in a long time. It howled again, though, closer this time. More coyote voices joined in. There was a pack of them! Evy was sure that if any critter had learned to survive, it would be a coyote. They were the most vivacious and well-adapting creatures on the planet. They scavenged for food and hunted in organized packs. They could survive on very little.

The howling was getting closer. Evy began to get nervous. She could not see anything with the sand blocking the moon and the cloud of dust that surrounded her. Bagby whinnied outside, but in truth was probably hollering for Myra to wake up. Clarence heard them, too. He scurried away, out of the tent and into a hole. He had found it on the side of a hill, the contents of which were probably little bones of a possum or armadillo. The thought made Evy shudder.

Myra awoke with a start. Her eyes were large. "Something found our trail. I can hear them talking. They are coming to eat us!"

Coyotes were messy things. Not very organized or sneaky at killing, but they were efficient. They were amazing trackers. And, they were coming for them. Myra lifted herself out of her sandy bed and Evy helped her rush to put the tent away. They piled their belongings onto the wagon. Then Myra locked Fluffy and his cage in a trunk to keep him safe.

Just as Bagby was about to be tied to the wagon, yellow eyes emerged in the swirling sand. A low rumbling growl echoed in the chilly air. Evy was terrified. Myra was using Bagby as a shield. She was always on self-preservation mode. Bagby was poised to fight. The coyotes crept closer and Evy looked around for a stick. Five of them emerged from the swirling sand.

"Straggly" would have been a nice way of describing them. They looked as though they were already dead. Their bones stuck out painfully through their skin and their matted, mangy fur clung tightly to it. A few of them were missing an ear or a tail. It had probably been eaten by one of its comrades when times had gotten too tough. It was a terrible thing to be the weakest in a pack.

They howled again and Myra lost her nerve. She jumped and ran, hollering as she went, up the bank and hill where Clarence was hiding. That set the chase! The coyotes lunged and Evy took off running, too, with Bagby trying to catch up. He could have easily passed Evy, but he put himself between the coyotes and her. The coyotes' sad state of being had made them somewhat slow, but even more dangerous and desperate.

Myra's long willowy legs carried her far ahead of them. She stopped, panting for breath in the thin air. She could not breathe with the mask on in the already sparse oxygen. She looked around at her surroundings. There was not much time.

She climbed up a small, rotting tree and wrapped her arms around it. It was the only one upright in the middle of a huge pasture. There was not enough room for Evy and definitely not enough for Bagby. Evy appeared over the hill running with heavy legs.

"Well, good luck to her." Myra mumbled, but was unconvinced in her mind. She fought her inner moral values. She wanted to live, but Evy was getting closer.

"Oh, fiddlesticks! I can't watch her die." Myra climbed down a little and wedged her foot in between a branch and the side of the tree to gain leverage. Then she held out her hand. Evy grabbed a hold of her hand and Myra heaved her up. As Bagby ran by, Myra leapt to his back so that Evy could climb up further. But Myra's foot had been wedged and it twisted with a loud crack. She hollered out in pain. The coyotes hollered back and continued their pursuit. Bagby sped up as a coyote leapt at him scratching at his purple behind.

Evy sat at the top of the tree panting heavily. A bony coyote with no ears was jumping at her on the ground, its yellow teeth glistening with saliva. Not far away another one was trying to dig Clarence out of his hole. Three of them were still chasing Myra and Bagby. Evy's mind had been so deprived of thought that she had forgotten her cursed triggers. Her spine was pulsing painfully alive with the magic inside her. She gave into it. Let it save her, once again.

Her body shook and morphed. She felt feathers burst through her skin. She hated that part, it was quite painful. Her face grew hard as a beak emerged from it. Two of her toes disappeared; which was a little scary. But it was worth it, she was a bird again, free and impossible to catch now. She was a beautiful red hawk. She spread her auburn wings wide and practiced a flap or two. Shut her eyes and leapt from the tree. The wind filled her feathers and lifted her. She rose higher and higher. When she was safely out of reach, she began to search the ground below for the others.

Bursts of purple lightning were shooting far below. Myra was blasting away at the ensuing coyotes. She would be okay for a moment. Clarence was in more dire need of assistance. She circled around and began to descend. The earless coyote had joined the other one now in digging for Clarence, having lost his first prey. They looked almost jubilant at the thought of eating again. Their tongues lolled out of their happy faces, and they dug vigorously. Clarence squealed in terror. Their claws were almost reaching him now. He turned around and positioned himself, lifted his tail and squeezed his purple buttocks. SQUIRT! A large, green cloud of sticky stench filled the hole and invaded the coyotes' noses.

They yelped and jumped backward, clawing at their noses and rolling in the sand. Evy lighted softly to the ground behind them and turned herself back to human. She found a large stick lying on the ground and then morphed invisible. She crept slowly up to them, raised her arms above her head and CRACK! She hit the first coyote with a thundering face plant. He lay dazed at her feet. The other coyote looked desperately around for their attacker, but saw no one. He could not sniff the air for fear of filling his lungs with sand. CRACK! Evy hit him in the side as hard as she could. He had no padding on his ribs and it was more than he could take. He tucked his tail and ran, whimpering into the wind.

She shimmered back to visible again and held her nose while she lifted Clarence out of the hole. "We need to go help Myra and Bagby. But, we need something that can move really fast." Clarence looked at her worriedly with his beady, little eyes. Evy was not sure how they could catch up with them. And then it dawned on her like a brilliant light bulb. "Clarence, get ready for something crazy."

Evy concentrated hard, willing herself to change. Her spine burned tired and weary, but the stress from their coyote battle was triggering her once again. She envisioned herself as what she wanted to turn into and her neck began to stretch and get longer. Her legs stretched, too. She sprouted large, red feathers. Perfect!

A giant ostrich stood before Clarence. "Hop on, buddy!" Evy clucked at him. She bent her long neck down so he could climb up. Once he was fastened tightly gripping her feathers, Evy took off. She ran so swiftly across the ground that it was hard to see where she was going. It was another freeing sensation close to flying. She spread her tiny, ostrich wings and felt the cool air ruffling her feathers. Clarence squealed with delight. Behind her, no-ears coyote had picked up the chase again, too desperate and hungry to give up.

They rounded a bend and headed for the purple lights ahead of them. Bagby and Myra were backed up against a large building. Myra was on her feet once again, and Bagby looked as though he would pass out at any moment.

The blasts of lightning were keeping the coyotes at bay, but they were getting more and more meager. Myra was getting tired. Evy was closing in fast, though. She just hoped she would be there in time before someone got bit or worse.

Myra was trying to talk sense into the wild, hungry coyotes, begging them for mercy in their own language. It was no use, of course; it did not even strike them as odd that she was able to speak to them. They were too desperate and too caught up in the moment to notice.

As Evy drew nearer, she noticed a light flickering inside the building. Tiny faces were pressing their noses to the upstairs window. There were children inside! "Myra, someone's in the building!" She hollered in her surprisingly squawky ostrich voice.

The pack of coyotes heard her too. They inched closer drooling at the thought of more people to eat. Evy reached the pack and kicked one of them as hard as she could in the behind. Her ostrich legs were strong and the coyote flew a few feet, landing with a thud.

No-ears had caught up with them and he snuck at her from behind. She let out another swift kick to another coyote, sending him flying also. Clarence clapped happily from her back chanting, "Kick 'em again! Kick 'em again!" She did not have time, though. No-ears lunged at her, biting a mouthful of her tail feathers. The last coyote standing used her moment of surprise as an opportunity and he jumped at her throat. Myra zapped him, sending him into spasmodic jerks on the ground.

Evy squawked loudly and took off running in circles with the coyote glued tightly to her tail and swinging in big loops behind her. His feet were flying behind him. No-ears found it kind of exhilarating. His bones hung lightly in the air twisting and bending. He ran his long tongue over her feathers. They tasted pretty good for feathers.

The door to the building opened a crack and someone's thick arm beckoned them in hurriedly. Myra and Bagby jumped through the door and Evy ran squawking towards it. The door was slammed shut in her face, however. So, Evy continued running from the coyotes and swinging No-ears while an argument ensued inside as to why they should let a skunk and an ostrich, let alone a donkey, into the building. Myra screamed and shouted at someone, while Bagby opened the door for Evy and Clarence.

Evy ran for the door with the exhausted coyotes still on her heels. She jumped and made it inside, slamming the door on her tail feathers and locking No-ears outside, still clamped down resolutely to her feathers. Clarence jumped lightly to the floor and Evy shook and morphed back to human, losing her feathers as she did.

The coyotes stood outside for the longest time. No-ears still clinging tightly to the feathers that he thought were connected to a bird. After a few hours, they sulked away sadly. Later, they happened across Myra and Evy's camp and the wagon and tore through it, devouring all the food inside. Fluffy had been lucky, having been locked inside the trunk thoughtfully by Myra. The thick walls and sandy air had prevented the coyotes from smelling him, and so, he had survived. Full and happy with the canned beans and homemade cornbread, the coyotes went on their merry way.

CHAPTER 12:
SWEET PIE

Myra and Evy were thrilled to find survivors. The strong chunky man who had opened the door for them had stopped his argument with Myra the second Evy had turned back to human. The portly man stood mouth agape for the longest time, however. Evy tried to look reassuring for him. "We come as friends. Thanks for saving our lives. We are Lippoliks. Do you know about Lippoliks?"

The man seemed to calm a moment. He nodded his head slowly. "I do, actually, and you are welcome. We had a lady roll through here once looking for survivors. I think her name was K Lippolik. She was a good woman with amazing powers. A few people went with her from our town, but we chose to stick it out. A few others joined the Snake Pirates, too. I've seen Lady K's powers and heard her tale. I've met more Lippoliks since then, too, and some were not as good as her, unfortunately."

Myra grew hopeful. "Have you met Jack Lippolik?"

"Actually, I have... more than once. He comes to my store to buy a few things every now and again. He has a son who lives down the road. If you need him, that's where I would look, but he's not too friendly that one. I'm not sure I would want to find him if I was you."

Evy jumped for joy. "Can you show us tomorrow where he lives? His son, I mean."

Buddy rubbed his forehead trying to decide if Myra and Evy meant him and his family harm. He concluded that he did not find them to be much of a threat. The donkey was rather big, though, but old. "I guess so...yes." Evy was thrilled. Myra suddenly looked a bit apprehensive. It had occurred to her that she did not know Jack had had a son and that bothered her immensely.

Evy looked around at the inside of the building. It was a mess. There were papers, cans and filthy clothes everywhere. Small, flickering candles were the only lights in the cavernous room. It appeared to be some sort of old grocery store. The shelves were gone, however, and the only reminders of its once grand disposition were the checkout counters lined up in the front. All of the conveyer belts had been made into beds for children to sleep on. There were ten in all. Each one still numbered by a giant white sign on a pole.

The man seemed to have concluded that they were indeed telling the truth, who else but a Lippolik could turn into a bird at will. He stared at Evy for a long time, her face looked familiar, but he could not figure out why. "Come on down kids, it's safe now," he called. Small, dirty faces appeared on a thin ladder leading up to the attic.

They began to descend like a long train. The oldest was sixteen and the youngest one looked like she was only two. There were ten little bodies, eleven people still alive. Evy felt her heart swell up with joy. They were messy and bedraggled, but they were alive. Buddy introduced his family to them.

"This is Amanda, Jacob, Norah, twins: Ben and Gordon, Meris, Bianca, twins: Pie and Sugar, and Lolli — which is short for Lollipop. My wife started to miss sweets there at the end of the country and after the Dead Water. Sugar does not keep well, I'm afraid. I feel bad for poor little Pie. Him being a boy, and all. Anyway, my name is Buddy. My wife Jessica is in bed, she is not well. Been sick for a long time." Buddy wiped a tear from his eye with a porky finger. "This is our home, and what used to be our business. So, now you know about us, tell us about yourselves."

Evy smiled at the children and waited for Myra to introduce her and their crew. But Myra was still mad about arguing with Buddy earlier and was trying to calm herself down. Her hair was flying around her head with static. The children were laughing and pointing at her. Evy cleared her throat, but Myra stood rigid with her arms crossed staring at the ceiling.

"I'm Evy. The crazy-haired lady is my Aunt Myra. The donkey's name is Doctor Bagby. And this is Clarence." She pointed at the skunk laying sprawled out on the floor taking heavy breaths.

Buddy nodded. "Did you say Doctor Bagby? Is he a Lippolik, too? Is he a real doctor?"

"Yes and no. He is not a Lippolik, but he is a real doctor. Although, he can't really do much doctoring anymore considering his predicament." Evy once again protected Myra from them by not revealing knowledge of her trigger. She was afraid that if people knew what she was capable of, they might hurt her. It was not entirely her fault, her triggers. Evy realized that for the first time and she felt a little pity for Myra. She did not like her yet, but she did not want to see her hurt.

"Oh," Buddy said, looking disappointed. "I was hoping he might be the answer to our prayers. My Jessica has been sick so long. I wish that the world was whole again so that I could take her to the best doctors, but I don't know how much longer she will live." Buddy burst into tears and his children surrounded him in a giant, family hug.

Myra lowered her arms and rolled her eyes at their public display of family affection. "I might be able to help her. Where is she?" Myra mumbled, trying to lessen the intensity of emotions.

Buddy's eyes lit up. "This way," he said enthusiastically, gesturing towards a large office area. Myra's torn ankle had already healed because of her trigger, which not only healed others but herself as well. She followed Buddy without a limp.

He led Myra to a small office overlooking the store. It had a large, one-way mirror next to a blind-drawn door. The sign on the door read, "Buddy Holder — Store Manager." He opened the door a crack and tiptoed carefully into the room. Myra followed less carefully and more on the noisy side.

As soon as their dad disappeared from sight into the office, the ten children jumped on Bagby whose legs where weak from running and he fell over on his side. He lay on the ground while the children climbed on him and pretended to ride him.

Jessica Holder lay deathly still in a large, padded bed. The bed's frame was made out of wooden pallets, which once held boxes of food. It was large and puffy. It swallowed her slight frame almost completely. Her eyes did not open as they entered the room, which was dimly lit by two small candles. On the walls around her were drawings of happier moments her children had given her. Her small, pixie face was beautiful and solemn. Her cheeks, however, were sunken and gray. Jessica's long, blonde hair lay frazzled in greasy locks around her face.

Myra shuddered. She had hoped that there was enough energy left in her to help, but considering the fight she had just endured, she was not sure. "How long has she been this way?" Myra asked. She was afraid of the answer, though. There was a time limit on her magic, unfortunately. She could heal things quicker if they had occurred within only moments of her arriving. Long-term illnesses were harder and more set than instant injuries. It was do-able though with the right supplies, which unfortunately, she did not have.

"It's been two months. Give or take a day," Buddy answered. His kind eyes implored her, begging for a solution. "Can you help her?"

Myra tried to smile reassuringly, but was not very good at it. She did not like to deal with hard things. "I might be able to help her, but I need to rest tonight."

"Don't you want to examine her or something?"

"Naw, I'm good. She looks pretty sick to me."

Buddy shook his head, confused. "Alright, let's find ya'll somewhere to sleep tonight then."

They walked out of the office and back into the store. Buddy dragged his children off of Bagby apologetically. Then he set about putting them to bed on their various conveyer belts. The four smaller children had to pair up and share a thin bed with each other in order that Myra and Evy might have one to sleep on. Myra's long legs hung off at the knees, but she did not complain much to Evy's great surprise. Myra's mind was too busy grouping together usable items into potions in her head that might save poor Jessica Holder. She considered it pure luck to have stumbled upon this opportunity, because it led them directly to Jack. She knew Buddy would be all too willing to help her find him if she cured his wife. Before she fell asleep, she kissed all her lucky charms that she had taken off of her neck and laid them beside her.

In the morning, they awoke with a start. Hot breath poured on their faces as small faces were gathered around them staring. A little, dirty boy who had been introduced as Pie carried a large tray precariously laden with food. The food consisted of mostly canned items and dried fruits, but it looked heavenly. He had a broad toothless grin and torn dirty clothes.

"I'm Pie. I'm four. Dad says Mom's not doing well today and that I'm to help you with anything you might need." His already broad grin grew impossibly larger. He was proud to be bestowed with such responsibility.

Myra rubbed her head and aching back. She sat up and stretched while the children stared. "I've wrestled with it all night. I can only think of a few ingredients that might work. I have two of them already. I just need canned hominy and a live growing flower. The last of which will be difficult to find considering it is winter and death outside. I'm not sure what to do about that. There's no substitute for that one really."

Pie started jumping up and down with his dirty hand raised in the air. His face looked blue as he held his breath in anticipation of being called upon. Myra watched him squirm with delight a few more moments. His enthusiasm was entertaining. "Yes, Pie? Do you have some news I need to know?"

Pie let out a long heavy breath and the color returned to his face. "I know where to get canned hominy," He heaved out between deep breaths.

"Oh, good. Lead the way then, Pie boy." Myra jumped elegantly from the conveyor bed and followed Pie to the back of the store. The long line of nine brothers and sisters followed them like a parade. Pie marched as though leading a marching band. Evy rolled into a ball to try and get a few more minutes of sleep.

Pie pushed through two large double doors that led to the store's storage room. Most of the large warehouse had been ravaged and torn apart. There was no food left, but there was a small door in the back, which Pie and his siblings uncovered behind a bunch of large shelves. It was the door to the basement.

"Dad says not to tell anyone about this door, because it's all the food we have. He says that someone might come and take our food away. Myra, are you gonna take our food away? You have to solemnly swear that you won't, or I can't show you the door (at this statement his oldest sister smacked herself in the head, because the deed had already been done)."

Myra raised her hand and swore. Pie seemed satisfied and he unlocked the door with a key his dad had given him. The steps down to the basement were dark and wet. A dank, moldy smell drifted up to greet them from below. They descended the slimy stairs carefully. At the bottom there were two small windows chiseled out of the concrete to let in the morning glow. Shelves, row upon row, stood tall and abundant in the morning's sunrays. They were filled with thousands of canned goods, dried fruits and packaged cereals. Large, bottled water pallets were stacked in the far right corner. Myra was amazed and jealous. They could survive for years if need be. It was a beautiful sight.

Lolli, the youngest baby girl, clung to Pie's leg sucking her thumb. He tried to hobble down the aisles to look for hominy, but it was slow progress with Lolli hanging on. The other children fanned out as well, anxious and grateful to have a chance at their mother back. It did not take long before Betsy hollered out that she had found it and they all ran up the aisles to join her in presenting the treasured canned good to Myra. They ascended the stairs once again and Pie locked the door behind them.

"Now, we need to find a flower." Myra paced up and down the width of the store and the children paced with her, giggling and stumbling over each other.

"Oh, for heaven's sake. Myra, you can't think of one living flower in the whole world," Evy grumbled, sitting up sorely from her hard bed. "Not one?" Myra looked at her dumbly shear anger burning in her eyes. She hated this game. It was the game where somebody knew the obvious answer to a question and it was not you and they made you feel stupid about it for two whole minutes, while you just stared at each other in silence. She never understood why people did that.

Myra did not break stare. She waited Evy out, getting annoyed all the while until red feathers began to pop out of Evy's skin due to Myra's annoyance. Evy began to be afraid of becoming a duck unwillingly again and gave up her game.

"Hyacinth Eichhornia Mycelium Improved. Our water filter flowers. They are back at the camp." Myra snapped her fingers, disappointed at herself. She was mostly upset that she had lost precious sleep over a very obvious answer.

Myra began to whine and complain about having to go and get it dramatically, until Evy gave in and went to fetch the wagon and flower with Bagby. It was a long walk back to their campsite. The morning air was icy and bitter. Their feet crunched on the frost-covered dirt at their feet. When they got closer they could hear Fluffy twittering angrily from his confines. The camp was an awful mess. Everything was torn to shreds. There were cans and blankets, clothes and broken glass everywhere.

One of the water jugs had been smashed, its precious flower trampled and squashed by the coyotes, but one had survived. Evy unlocked the trunk and got Fluffy and his cage out. She fed him some dried raisins from the grocery store. Then she set about gathering what was left of their belongings. She folded the tent and put it in first. Then she gathered Myra's fancy bloomers. Lastly, she put the flower still in the jar next to Fluffy on top of the wagon. She then hitched the wagon onto Bagby and they headed back. She felt a little guilty about the littered mess she left behind, but what was she going to do, throw it away?

When they arrived back at the store, Myra's health potion was already mashed and ready. It was boiling on a small fire she had made Clarence gather outside and he was dancing around it like an Indian. She looked painfully at the flower in the jar that Evy had brought her and cut a branch with buds off of it carefully. Myra dropped it into the pot and stirred. She stepped back and pointed her pinky finger at the boiling concoction. ZAP! The pot bubbled over, spilling the mixture onto the fire where it melted a log. Amanda, the oldest Holder child, gulped. She had been watching Myra closely. "Is it going to melt my mama?" She asked, worried.

Myra shrugged, unconcerned. She poured some of the mixture into a small, glass jar and set it down on the cold ground to cool. When it had cooled, she spread the mixture on to a flat rock where it hardened and then cut it into strips. She whistled while she rolled these strips into five ball-like pills.

"There, now make sure she takes one a day for five days. Don't let her skip one at any cost. Do you understand? Alright, now who is gonna take us to Jack's son's house?"

Amanda took the pills worriedly. She had just seen the formula melt a log and she was in no hurry to let Myra walk away forever having melted her mama.

"Let's go and make sure these work before ya'll go disappearing into the night, shall we? If they don't, you're still our best shot to cure her, and if they melt her...well, Daddy's gonna be mad. You'll have heck to pay if she dies."

Myra sighed loudly and dramatically. They followed Amanda inside to her mother's room, Myra mumbling angrily the whole way under her breath about ungratefulness. They entered her room just as Myra was getting to the part where she sarcastically threw her arms into the air and proclaimed, "It's not as if we are on a mission to save the world, let's make sure this saves my mama first. Sheesh! Go ahead; we have all the time in the world." She stood in the corner tapping her foot impatiently, her hair flying statically around her angry eyes. Evy ran to calm her before someone else became a duck, or worse.

Amanda poured her mom some water from the table next to her and put a pill into her mouth. They all waited with eager breaths. Jessica Holder's eyes slowly opened. She looked wearily around the room. While they watched, her eyes turned from green to purple. Her face grew less gray and she smiled.

Amanda screamed with joy and threw her arms around her tearful dad. Buddy got up off his chair and embraced his wife as he cried like a giant baby. Evy turned to congratulate Myra, but she had left the room, overwhelmed and annoyed by the emotion inside it. Evy gave Myra a pat on the back, in her mind, and went to find her.

She was outside hooking Bagby up to the wagon once again. Her hair was calmer, but she looked determined. Pie ran through the door and grabbed Myra around her knees almost knocking her over. His dirty face was washed with his tears. "Thank you, Myra! Thank you, you're my hero."

Evy saw a flash of tenderness in her face for one second and then it was gone. She pried Pie from her legs and lifted his dirty face in her hands. "Take me to Jack." Pie nodded, his fat cheeks were bunched together giving him fishy lips. She let go of his face and he ran inside to ask his dad. When he came back outside, he was with his sister, Amanda.

"My dad says Godspeed and thank you! We will be forever in your debt. My mama is doing so much better already. Pie and I will take you to Robert Lippolik's house. The other children don't wanna leave mama's side," Amanda said.

Myra sighed. "Well it's about time. I am anxious to meet this Robert. I really gotta get out more. I can't believe, I didn't know about him."

They loaded a few canned goods from the store basement onto the wagon. Then they lifted up Clarence and Pie into the wagon and began walking towards town.

It was a windy day. The sun was hidden by the clouds and sand swirled around them scratching at their faces. The road was buried in the sand long ago, but the houses were lined in perfect rows along its phantom path, so it was easy to know that they were still on it. They passed row after row of silent houses lying crumbled around them. Ahead they could see the strangest sight. It loomed through the sand like a mirage. At first, Evy could not believe it. It had been almost a week since she had seen one, let alone many. She blinked and strained her eyes to look ahead. Myra, too, looked confused. Amanda poked Evy in the ribs. "I know, I was awed, too, the first time I saw it."

"Trees! A whole forest of trees with actual leaves! But, how? How did they survive?" Evy felt close to tears at the sight of them.

Amanda shook her head. "I don't know. It's a miracle, that's for sure." The trees were mostly pine. Green and plush, they stood tall against the horizon. Amanda stopped walking. "Well now you know where you are going now. So, I think Pie and I should be heading back. I think Robert's house is right there on the edge. I've heard tales that Jack's house is hidden in the top of a tree camouflaged. Good luck and thanks again!" Amanda lifted Pie from the wagon. Pie waved goodbye enthusiastically as they headed back the way they had come.

There was a small, log house sitting on the edge of the forest when they got closer. Its windows were shaded and dark. It blended into the trees behind it making it hard to see. Myra went and knocked. There was a loud scuffling noise inside and someone peered through the window at them. More scuffling and then a tall blonde man answered the door. He was entirely too thin, but his features were sharp and handsome. He had perfect, movie star teeth, clean clothes and his hair was combed neatly to one side.

"Yes?" He asked, peering at them in a very non-friendly way.

Myra took a step back. "Well, you look just like him. Can we come in? I'm your Aunt. My name is Myra and this is your cousin Evy."

Robert frowned. "I'm a little busy right now. What did you say your name was again?"

"You heard me," Myra shot back. "Where's Jack?" Myra pushed her way inside the house. The house was dark and empty. A large waxy candle sat on a wooden table filled with food. There were two plates — two steaming plates. "Is he here? Jack, come out to face me you coward!" No one came.

Robert looked pleased. "No one is here, but me, madam. Now if you don't mind I would like to get back to my dinner." He shoved her roughly to the door. Myra shocked him with her electric bursts on the arm, though, and he let go with a jump. Robert smiled deviously and rubbed his sore, red arm.

"My dad's not here. He was called away at last second, but he would have liked to meet you. I know a few tricks myself, wanna see?" Myra did not want to see, but he closed his eyes anyhow. He was remembering something, a moment that made him feel a certain emotion. His body began to shake and trigger. He popped open his eyes and laughed. It was a wild hideous laugh, unbridled and crazy. The laugh grew louder and shriller. Myra unconsciously touched her fingers to her head and Poof! All her beautiful, blonde hair fell out of her head into a pile on the floor. Her eyebrow hair was gone, too. Every hair on her body had taken a suicidal dive from its pore. Robert laughed more wildly than ever.

Myra was annoyed! Very annoyed! Her eyes looked a bit scary and Evy backed away from the open door. Robert's hair on the back of his neck began to stand on end. A look of panic crossed his face. "I'll put it back! I'll put it back!" He yelled. He closed his eyes, concentrating. Myra's hair began to grow, but it was too late. CRACK! Robert suddenly crouched before her, a pink, hairless pig with a purple butt. The smoky air smelled like bacon.

"Myra, no! Why did you do that? Now we won't be able to find Jack and if we do, he's gonna get so mad." Evy was horrified. Myra calmed down. Her hair was spiky and short now with a hint of orange tips, because Robert had not gotten to finish growing it back.

Robert the pig was running wildly around the room, upturning chairs and tables. "It was an accident. I've been holding back for days. He pushed me to it." Myra tried hard to justify it, but deep down, she knew she had gone too far.

CHAPTER 13:

JACK

Myra closed the cabin door. They stepped outside under the shadow of the glorious trees. Hanging her head in shame, she walked over to their wagon. Clarence and Bagby turned their faces away from her. Evy was mad at her for her lack of self-control as well. Myra had ruined everyone's chances at getting Jack on their side in one fell swoop of annoyance.

They headed into the shelter of the trees, unsure of how to proceed. It was a deep, thick forest. The sound of Robert the Pig echoed loudly behind them as he continued squealing and breaking things. They wandered aimlessly away, hoping to stumble across something, anything and unsure of what to do next. The squealing stopped behind them finally.

Ahead of them, a large lake two miles in diameter stretched icky and green before them. It was definitely poisoned, but the trees were alive none the less. A small island rose in the middle of the lake, big enough for only one tree which grew tall in its center.

Something sparkled in its branches. The sun was shining down on the windows of Jack's house. It caught them just so. Without the glittering windows, it would have been impossible to spot.

"How are we gonna get over there?" Evy asked. "If we touch the water we are dead and I don't see a boat anywhere."

"Do you think it's wise for us to still go see him after what I've done?"

"What choice do we have? He doesn't know yet. I'll try to think of something to fix Robert while you talk to him. Maybe my bracelet can fix him. Mom said it would protect me from you."

"And pray tell, how am I supposed to get over there?" Myra asked. "You're the bird, remember. You can fly there. You're the only one who can get across the water."

"Oh, yeah." Evy kept forgetting. She set her weary mind to think of her mom. The thought made her emotional and she felt her spine begin to pulse. She pictured a bird in her mind like she had been doing lately. It froze there, as a blueprint, and she felt herself morphing. Feathers popped through her skin and wings replaced her arms. She shrunk and squeezed into a tinier form. She was suddenly a tiny bluebird with a red head.

She whistled in glee, then spread her tiny wings and pushed off from the ground. It was the easiest flight yet. She soared across the dark, green waters and tried not to look down at them, but focused instead on the tree ahead of her.

It grew larger and grander as she drew nearer. It was as big as a redwood tree that she had seen on a vacation with her mom when she was a little girl. Its branches were sturdy and thick, strong enough to support the large cabin nestled atop them. Its jaded needles blocked the view of most of the house. There were no ladders up to it or doors on the house's frame. It was just a large wooden box with windows. Evy remembered Myra saying, that Jack could teleport.

"I guess he doesn't need doors," Evy thought aloud, but could not figure out how to get herself in. Then, she saw a chimney. She flew down it and into what must have been the living room.

The room was tidy and mannish. All the colors were washed-out variants of brown. The chairs were homemade out of strange-looking leather. There were wooden chairs and small wooden tables. Evy fluttered and lighted on the back of a wooden chair. A small desk sat in the corner.

Jewelry was piled high on its glossy surface. There were at least ten different ornate pieces. They were spread about and labeled with tags as if they were part of a study. Evy flew closer. It appeared that these were of the same age as Evy's bracelet. But, how did he get so many when Lippoliks only receive one on their thirteenth birthday? She absentmindedly touched the bracelet still hanging on her left wing.

The tags on them were names. Evy gasped! They were the names of family members: Woody, Aunt Johnny, Aunt Pete, Aunt Mary, Annalisa, Uncle Sean, Eddie, Marten, Evelyn and Myra... Myra's long lost jewelry was labeled and stacked with the rest. It was a brooch made of purple amethyst and shaped like a hippo. It was whimsical and heavy, probably worth a fortune. Evy felt a vibrating Boom, shake the kitchen. The house shook and the needles rattled outside. Dust fell from the rafters and some birds took flight from the branches of the great tree, twittering in annoyance.

Jack was home! Evy did not know what to do. She had some things she needed to sort out now before she talked to him. Like for instance, why he had other people's jewelry? She was not sure which side he was on now. She picked up Myra's jewelry from the pile with her beak and flew back up the chimney.

She flew across the water as fast as her tiny wings would carry her. "Myra, we have to hide!" She tweeted when she reached them. She accidentally dropped the brooch as she said it.

"Jack's home and I don't think he's on our side." Myra reached down and picked up the brooch with revulsion. She thought she would never see it again and good riddance. She stuffed it into her pocket so she could throw it away somewhere safe forever and then urged Bagby to run.

Across the lake, up in the tree, Jack had already seen them. He peered with ashen gray eyes at their desperate scramble to hide and then BOOM, disappeared.

Myra, Evy, Bagby and Clarence kept running for a long while until they could run no more. They were deep in the forest and it was getting late. Myra was pretty sure Jack had not followed them, because if he had he would catch them easily by teleporting. They set up camp, but no campfire. Just to be safe. They fell asleep to the whistling sand through the trees.

Dark shadows blocked the morning sun's rays from filtering through the opaque tent walls. Loud whispers in honks, squeaks and barks awoke Evy with their twaddle. The sand had formed hard, crispy crust on her eyes, however. She did not see the shadows encircling, but she heard them. It was a strong disadvantage of having incredible hearing. She could hear too well and the noise never stopped, especially when you were trying to sleep.

The noise around her was chaotic and excitable. She rubbed her sore eyes hard to remove the sand from them. Her eyes felt raw as if they had just been scrubbed with sandpaper.

"Ridiculous," She whispered, upon seeing Myra still asleep with all the noise. Myra's muffled snoring through her mask was still extremely loud beside her and Clarence was nowhere to be seen. The voices outside hushed when she sat up. "Huh," she thought, "Not very subtle." Evy knew they were probably in extreme danger.

The shadows outside moved to a more hunkered down position. Evy began to feel nervous. Her spine began to tingle. She elbowed Myra hard in the ribs and Myra sat up with her arms swinging. She would have landed a pretty hard punch to the face if Evy had not ducked quickly.

"There are animals outside. What do we do?" Myra rubbed her swollen eyes as well and looked around.

"They came here to get us, I'm sure. And I say, not without a fight!" On that note, Myra charged at them, sand streaming behind her, out of the tent and straight for the crowd of shadows outside.

Evy felt her spine began to pulse and she triggered into a griffin once again. Feathers erupted through her skin pores. A tail grew from her behind. Her talons tore through the thin tent walls and she emerged like a raging butterfly from a chrysalis. Myra stood like a giant dirtball, energetically zapping the animals with her electric bursts, which only seemed to anger them more.

"What more could you do to us," they screamed and they jumped on her from every angle, forcing her to the dirty ground. Evy lunged at them, but the kangaroo caught her in mid-air with a swift kick to the face, knocking her out cold. She writhed on the ground as her body turned back in to human. Then she was still.

The other animals lost their hold of Myra and she raced for Bagby, who had been tied tightly to a large boulder. She ran to the wagon beside him and grabbed Fluffy the pigeon's cage from it. She whispered into Fluffy's ear and opened the cage door. He flew out faster than anything the animals had ever seen before. He was gone in just a few seconds and no one could stop him.

Then they jumped Myra again. This time she was too tired to fight. She gave in and let them tie her up. They put her in the back of the wagon and tied it to the black horse with the painted lips. Bagby was tied to the back of the wagon, too, and even though he protested, the horse was much stronger and won.

Gracie, the translator for Rufus the Possum, got out of a green Cadillac car parked above the cliff and walked slowly towards Evy and the crowd of animals. She pulled a lollipop from her tiny mouth and looked at Rufus with her beady, green eyes. "Well done, Rat. My cousin will be pleased."

"I told you, I'm not a rat!" he protested, but his glory in victory made him wave the insult away. He did not care what she called him, because he would be called "human" again soon. "She's all yours," he said, pointing at the still unconscious Evy.

He rubbed his tiny paws together excitedly and headed back to the crowd of cheering animals. The animals headed back to the P.B.U. with Myra, who was still zapping one or two of them randomly the whole way with malice in her eyes.

The bodyguard got out of the car, too, and picked up Evy's limp, human body. He carried her to the car and laid her into the back seat. Gracie climbed in beside her and shut the door.

"Let's go, Billy." The bodyguard flinched at the sound of his name. He did not think she knew it. He started the car and pulled onto the highway.

Evy moaned and opened her eyes. It felt like her face was on fire. Gracie sat next to her listening to her headphones motionless. She turned her green eyes on Evy and a shiver ran down Evy's spine.

"Oh, so you're awake, huh? Don't try anything or Billy will just have to shoot you. The King said dead or alive, so..." She turned the music back on. Evy rubbed her forehead. She was so mad that feathers were popping up through her hair, which incidentally only made her headache worse.   Her sore eyes glanced at her surroundings.   The dark-haired girl sat staring out the window beside her. Evy studied her pale face.

She recognized Gracie by her familiar look, but just barely. She looked just like Uncle Woody, the spitting image of her father, actually. Evy did not know he had had a daughter, but then again she had missed a lot so it would not surprise her. Gracie had not grown up well, though, apparently. Oh, she was pretty enough in a dark and evil way, but Evy could tell she enjoyed this adventurous evil a little too much. Her heart was not as kind as her father's or mother's had been. Evy could see it in her eyes.

"My mom is going to come and save me. She, Jack and Uncle Woody will come to get you," Evy bluffed, hoping Gracie would buy it.

Gracie scoffed. "Who do you think tipped us off? Jack doesn't like to be found. He's always been a big help to the King. Oh yeah, and Uncle Woody, my dad, (she stressed the dad part) is dead."

Evy's heart skipped a beat. Uncle Woody was dead? "How did he die?!"

"My dad's trigger was water and he couldn't stay out of it. He was one of the first to die."

"Poor Uncle Woody...I guess that makes sense. I always thought his pipe smoke looked more like steam than smoke, really. I miss him already." Tears fell down Evy's dirty face. She had hoped the labeled jewelry she had found had been stolen not taken from the dead hands of her family members. She cried for them and for herself. The King obviously wanted her dead so he could steal her bracelet, too. She wondered if it would give him powers to turn into a bird, too. Her tears turned to sobs and Gracie squirmed uncomfortably beside her.

"Seriously! I want to ride the rest of the way in peace, just listening to my music!" And with that, Gracie wiggled her black-tipped fingers at Evy and Evy was silenced. She grabbed at her mute throat. She screamed, but it was only hot air that brushed her lips. Her eyes widened in panic. She triggered, faded and turned invisible.

"Well, what do you know; she can turn invisible, too. Good for you," Gracie said humdrum. "All right, I'll give you back your speech if you make yourself visible again. Huh? Deal?" Gracie put her arm into the seat next to her to feel for Evy. She was not there. Gracie panicked.

"Come on! He'll kill me if I don't bring you back. Please!"

Evy did not want to stay mute forever, nor did she want anyone killed on her behalf so she calmed herself and decided to become visible again. Maybe, she could figure out a plan to escape later. She shimmered and reappeared.

Gracie wiggled her fingers at her again and gave her back her voice. "Thanks." Evy said and waited a moment for her to say something — anything in return, but Gracie just put her headphones back on and stared out the window. Evy felt a little sorry for her. She could not be much older than herself, maybe sixteen. She wondered how she had gotten mixed up in all this.

Evy was worried about Myra, too. She hoped that the animals would show her mercy. And where was Clarence? She hoped he was okay wherever he was. They rode in silence. Evy left to her dreadful thoughts. She rubbed her bracelet clasped to her wrist and wondered if it was the last time she would wear it.

A sprawling, broken city emerged in the distance. Its tall skyscrapers were unkempt and haggard and most of the windows in them were gone. Everything had a gray skin covering it, like a melancholy blanket. The buildings sagged under their unmanaged weight drearily, as if depressed. They were rusted with sand-crusted floors. They had endured thousands of pounding sandstorms night after night. The city was in ruins. Evy remembered the city as it was before, bustling and colorful. Without people, it was just a shell. They drove across an antique bridge carpeted in sand and off an exit to the right. Dead rusty cars lay tossed and shoved to the side of the road.

A black, skinny building with a ball tower built on top, loomed ahead of them. Its glossy surface was well-maintained. It was Kallon's home, Evy knew it. It was the only building not broken. Evy's stomach began to do flip-flops. She was having trouble staying visible, because she was so nervous and Gracie kept giving her heated looks.

A crowd was gathered outside the doors to the building. There were a lot of hooligans laughing and punching at each other with glee. One man stood confidently waiting, dressed in a black jacket and green t-shirt. He looked like John, but Evy had to remind herself that he was dead.

On his head, he wore an intricate crown carved with fine filigree and with large diamonds set into its facets. "Much too fancy to be worn with a t-shirt," Evy thought and it made him less frightening somehow for his lack of style. It was a thought that made Evy laugh out loud. Now that he was no longer scary to her, the facade of John fell like liquid pouring from Kallon's face and Evy saw Kallon's true face for the first time. Part of her heart went out to him, as soon as she saw him. She wished she could have been in his life to influence and change him. She loved him instantly, because he was her brother. On the outside he shared a lot of her mother's features, too, which added to her feelings for him. He had the dark hair, her mother's chiseled cheeks and cleft chin. He was beautiful on the outside, but Evy also knew what was behind his black eyes. He was ugly inside and it made her sad.

The green Cadillac came to a stop and Billy the bodyguard got out and walked around the side of the car. He opened the door for Gracie and grabbed Evy's arm roughly to pull her out. Kallon sauntered with sure strides over to Evy, eyeing her up and down. A small smile played on his lips. The crowd of goons behind him pressed forward to get a better look at the griffin girl. Kallon's eyes locked firmly on Evy's bracelet. He reached a hand out to touch it, but Evy jerked her hand away.

"It's beautiful. Where did you get it?" he asked, knowing full well the answer. Evy did not answer, but stared hard at the ground. "Can I have it?" Kallon had to stifle a laugh at his own joke. Evy's eyes met his and she shook her head resolutely no. "Very well then, you're not the first Lippolik to resist, I'm afraid." Having said his piece, he lifted her head and spit in her face. "Resist that!"

He smiled again, pure joyous hate lighting up his eyes. Evy trembled and convulsed. She fell before him writhing in pain. It felt like her whole body was on fire. "What is happening?" she thought. Her hands turned green and withered in front of her face. She felt her muscles constrict and fold her body unwillingly. She imagined herself looking like the crumbled guard she had seen outside Mrs. Eldran's classroom the first time she had seen Kallon.

A horrible realization dawned in her mind right before she went into a painful slumberous shutdown. His spit was poisonous, the poison that must have caused it all. All the death and all the pain was caused by a little spit and an evil heart. He must have duplicated his spit somehow. That must be how he had killed the guard next to their door that night at the refugee school and how he had caught him by surprise. It must be what was poisoning the rivers, too. Her mind was burning with questions and pain. She felt like it would explode at any moment. She fought it, tried to purge herself of it.

Then a warm sensation washed up her arm. It soothed the pain like a warm washcloth. The pain pulsed on, but somewhere below her mind she felt a sense of peace as her arm burned hot and heavy with pulsing waves of growing strength. Her bracelet was throbbing, trying to save her. She felt Kallon rip it from her wrist and then she fell, collapsing like a small sputtering fire.

CHAPTER 14:

THE P.B.U'S REVENGE

Myra blinked. She was dizzy from the energy she had zapped herself of trying to fight the animals off for a whole day. Bagby was no longer struggling to drag himself behind the wagon, either. He had been trying to add strain to the lady horse by pulling it in the opposite direction. Consequently, he was worn out, too. Myra lay down atop the tent and closed her eyes.

She knew once they got to their destination she was dead. It was unavoidable really. Her life had led up to this moment all along. She just hoped that Kyla could get to Evy in time to save her, or else Evy would share her fate. She hoped that Fluffy had made it to Kyla with her message.

The band of animal morphs moved along steadily towards the horizon. The overjoyed critters were singing some sort of "Revenge is Sweet" ballad that they had undoubtedly practiced many times at the top of their lungs.

The P.B.U loomed dark and dreary in the distance. It grew larger and so did the fear in the pit of Myra's stomach. The lady horse stopped walking at the entrance to the large barn. The larger animals tied Bagby to a post despite his adamant protest. Then they drug Myra from the wagon and inside the door. Rufus ordered them to tie Myra to a chair.

"Well, well, well…I've been waiting for this a long time, Myra," Rufus hissed. The crowd behind him echoed in agreement. He stood on a chair in front of her so that he could be eye to eye with her. He stretched his arms out and cracked his knuckles. Then he reared back and scratched Myra across the face with his yellow claws.

Myra let a tear fall down her torn cheek. It began to mend right away, though, leaving only streaks of blood where the scratches had been.

"Oh, goody. We can do this all night," Rufus murmured as he reared back to scratch her again.

Myra stared back at him with a feeling of irritation beginning to grow. "I'm sure you have been waiting for this a long time, Rufus. Although, it is my opinion that that animal suit seems to compliment your eyes. Besides, you were one of the few that I turned with good reason."

"I hardly think that anyone would deserve such a punishment. Who made you the judge?" One animal yelled from the crowd. Rufus curled his lips back revealing his tiny, sharp teeth.

The barn erupted in enthusiastic agreement. Rufus looked pleased. "Oh, but Rufus, dear, why don't you let your comrades here be the judges then. Tell them what you did and if they don't think you deserved it, I'll simply turn you back."

Everyone got quiet. Rufus became flustered. "You said you couldn't fix this. You told me when you turned me that it was permanent!"

Myra smiled genuinely. "It **was** permanent. I've since found the cure. You've seen it for yourself, actually." She looked around the room, as loud whispering rumbled through it. "Oh, I guess he didn't tell ya'll. Evy, my companion, used to be a duck, but I changed her back. It's a game we play now whenever she feels like it. I turned her into that griffin you saw as well. Then I turned her back. It's great fun." Myra glanced around the room again to see if they were buying it. A few of them looked at Rufus, beseeching him with their eyes.

"Change me back then, I demand it. Change us all back!" he yelled, spittle splashing on Myra's face.

Myra shook her head. "Only if you tell them all why I changed you!" Myra yelled back. Rufus growled. There was no way he was going to tell them. He knew that they would not side with him anymore and he was happy being their leader.

"I don't have to! We have lived like this for far too long and we deserve our lives back!"

To Rufus' huge delight the room echoed his agreement with a loud uproar. They began to chant, "Change us back! Change us back! Change us back!"

Myra looked around the room blearily, lost for words. She had hoped that the others finding out his history would be enough to turn them on Rufus. She looked around at their faces. They would never believe her if she told them herself so she changed her strategy.

"Why should I change you back just so you can kill my family? I would be signing their death warrants. You have all helped spy for the King for many years. If you did not deserve it then, you definitely do now." The room grew silent. Many of them hung their heads in shame, lost in thought. Myra continued, "You have stayed loyal to a king who has killed your families, your friends and is now after mine! You've let your revenge turn you into bitter servants of a murderous king. Don't get me wrong, I do owe you. I deserve punishment, indeed, but so do you! You are no better than me now. You have lowered yourselves in order that you might have revenge! Was it worth it? When you are human again, who will you go home too?"

The animals began to argue with one another. The ones who had been turned for good reason, suddenly stood out from those who had not. Their stories began to be passed among them. The stories of how each had come to know Myra. They had been told in that barn many times already and everyone knew everyone else's story. They began to blame each other. Bitter fighting erupted in the back corner by the bar.

A chair flew at the kangaroo who had rudely told a sheep that he deserved to stay that way. Then the kangaroo kicked out at the sheep with his gigantic foot and missed, knocking a pig's tooth out and sending a squirrel flying across the room. The kangaroo's friend, the lady horse, jumped on the sheep and his three buddies. It did not take long for it to become an all out war.

Rufus jumped from his chair angrily. He tried to stop the fight, but received a hard punch to the stomach for his efforts. He grabbed one of the pig's legs, pulled hard and knocked him to the ground. Then he whispered into his ear. Together they drug Myra, still tied to the chair, out the back door. Rufus ordered the pig to grab a shovel.

"Myra, I will be more than happy to kill you right here. It is gonna take a lot of choice words to undo that mess you just made in there. You've done enough talking, now, change me back!"

"Never!" Myra shouted. Rufus rolled his eyes and ran his finger across his neck for the pig to see. The pig reared back ready to hit Myra with the shovel. Myra wiggled and jumped in her chair, trying not to be an easy target to hit. As she did, something shiny fell from her pocket.

The amethyst, hippo brooch lay glittering on the ground in the moonlight. "Wait!" Rufus hollered, staying the deadly strike with his hand. He reached down carefully for the brooch. His eyes were glowing with greed. As soon as he touched it, his body began to shake. His eyes rolled back and his teeth clattered together. He twisted and flickered, growing in size. The hair from his face fell like a shiny waterfall to the ground. Rufus turned back to human! His hair was rough, messy and gray. He had a long, sharp nose and buckteeth. It occurred to the pig, at that point, that perhaps Myra was right when she had said that Rufus was much better looking as a possum.

The pig dropped the shovel and stood staring open-mouthed. He shook his head and looked in awe at the large, gray-haired man standing before him. How had he fit inside such a little possum body?

The pig squealed excitedly and reached for the brooch. Rufus laughed deeply and jerked it away from him. He twisted left, fell on the ground and rolled for the shovel. Then he lifted it up and struck the pig on the head. The pig fell bleeding to the ground. He was dead.

The fighting inside the P.B.U was getting louder. Rufus snuck around the front of the barn and untied Bagby, who whinnied and pulled in protest. Rufus drug him around the back to Myra.

"I can't let the King lose his animal army. I don't want them to know about this brooch. They are going to think you killed the pig. At least that's what I'm going to tell them. I'll tell them that the King in his mightiness turned me back to human as a reward for finding Evy. I'm taking this back to the King. (He held up the brooch) There is a great reward for finding one of these." Rufus laughed with a booming manly voice. "So long, Myra!" He untied her hands and she slapped him hard across the face. "I would get going if I were you," he sneered, while he rubbed his bruised cheek. And then he disappeared into the sandy night.

Bagby looked at Myra with his large, watery eyes. "What do we do? Is that all it took to turn me back?" He asked.

Myra nodded and shrugged. "I guess so. We better get out of here. We need to follow Rufus to Kallon's hideout so we can get that brooch back and save Evy."

Bagby nodded and they headed out after Rufus. The P.B.U. was crashing and banging loudly behind them. Up in the loft window, however, a small Chihuahua with green paws watched Myra disappear into the night. She waved her tiny paw in farewell at Myra's disappearing form and wished her well. It was up to her now. The Chihuahua had to end this. Then she climbed down to the floor with a plan to win a war.

CHAPTER 15:

BIG PAPA

They thought she was dead. She was not moving and her whole body was a faded, green color. The King's bodyguards lifted Evy's lifeless form and took her around the back of the building. They swung her into a large pile of trash on the count of three, dusted off their hands and walked away.

She laid there unmoving, unfeeling and hope began to fade away. Her mind was still alive, though, somehow. It had clicked on almost as soon as the guards left. It was still providing her with basic functions like breathing, heart beats and sweat. The trash stunk, but Evy did not smell it. Her mind was still trying to get that function back.

After three days of lying in the trash barely functioning, Clarence found her. He had gone back to get help from Buddy Holder at the grocery store when the P.B.U. had jumped Myra and Evy. He and Buddy had been looking for them for days.

They, too, thought that it was too late when they finally happened upon her lying in the trash in the middle of the night. Clarence burst out sobbing. Buddy patted him sympathetically on the back. Evy heard them, but she could do nothing about it except lay there pathetically. The poison had paralyzed her, but the bracelet had saved her up until it had been ripped from her arm. She needed Myra to heal her, but Myra was busy escaping from the P.B.U. hours from where Evy was.

Clarence lay sobbing on the stinky trash. His loud crying was going to earn the attention of the King soon so Buddy stifled him kindly. His sobs were drowned luckily, however, by his face mask and the sand beating on the windows. He pulled himself together and held Evy's hand in his tiny paw. Evy reflexively squeezed back!

She was alive! Clarence jumped up dancing. "What happened?" Buddy asked.

"She squeezed my hand!" Clarence shouted in his squeaky, skunk voice and then continued dancing salsa-style. "She's alive!"

Buddy shook his head, not understanding the excited squeaks that Clarence was making. Clarence had had to write the words on paper when he had come for Buddy, so that he would understand that Evy and Myra had gotten kidnapped. Something was exciting the skunk, though. Buddy studied Evy's face.

He felt for a pulse and found one, faint but steady. She was alive! He understood now why Clarence was dancing. He lifted Evy up carefully and searched the surroundings for shelter from the howling sand. There was a manhole twenty feet away. He pried open the lid and they climbed down the metal ladder. The howling sandstorm was much quieter at the bottom. Buddy found a nice, cool corner and he laid Evy down.

"I wish Myra was here," Buddy whispered as he bent and wiped some sand from Evy's green face. "My wife is healthier now than she has been in twenty years. Myra could save Evy, no problem." Candlelight flashed down the left tunnel and they heard guards coming from it, laughing and making their rounds.

"We have to keep moving," Buddy whispered. He lifted Evy again and they took the tunnel to the right, moving like shadows. The sewer was not like it used to be twenty years or so ago. It still smelled something terrible, but it was dry as a bone. It was cold and crypt-like. They dodged more guards and headed down another tunnel, turning left or right again and again. Pretty soon, they were completely lost.

At the end of a large vast tunnel, they saw two guards playing poker on a low, wooden table. Large sconces holding torches lined the walls. Behind the guards, there were large, metal bars functioning as a prison. Men, women and children opposed to the King in some form or way lay scattered on the revolting floor. Their clothes were tattered. Their faces dirty. The only reason they were kept alive was to entertain the King's tortuous desires.

One of the prisoners, an old man, sat on a rock behind bars playing the card game with the prison guards. The light from the torches illuminated his wrinkle-lined face. Clarence recognized him immediately. It was Big Papa. Clarence had met him once, a long time ago. It had been on his last night as a human, the night he had picked Myra up for a date. Bad memories began to creep their way into his mind. He threw them out. He focused instead on the task at hand. He knew that Big Papa could fix Evy, too. Myra said he was a healer, but how could they get her to him? How could he get Buddy to understand that he should take Evy to him?

Buddy started to turn around with Evy in his giant arms and go down the tunnel behind him to avoid the guards, but Clarence stopped him. He jumped in front of him waving his arms.

Clarence wrote "healer" with an arrow in the dirt that pointed to the prison cell. Buddy nodded and understood. Now, all they needed was a diversion for the guards. Clarence sat down on a low-lying tunnel's edge to think. Buddy understood, too, that they needed some way to get past the guards.

It was probably one of the luckiest breaks ever. Suddenly, a loud noise rumbled above their heads. The sewer walls shivered and pieces of stone and mortar rained on their heads. The noise rumbled again, louder. It shook the walls like a huge hurricane.

The guards at the table stood and dropped their cards. A desperate high-pitched voice sounded over their walkie-talkies. The guards looked at each other with fearful eyes and then ran up the tunnel towards Clarence and Buddy.

Clarence and Buddy ducked into the low tunnel just in time, melding with shadows. The boots of the guards echoed loudly down the tunnel away from them. The rumbling above them was getting louder. Clarence was worried that the tunnel would collapse on their heads.

Buddy lifted Evy and carried her towards the jail cell. They would not have much time before the guards might come back. Big Papa stood from his rock chair as they entered the light of the sconces on the walls. His hand flew to his chest and tears welled in his eyes.

"I've not seen her in 20 something years. Evy looks the same. She was less green, of course, but I know that that is my Evy. We thought her dead many years ago. Bring her here! Bring her here." He reached his dirty arms through the bars for his granddaughter. A handsome, dirty-faced man stood up in the back of the cell. His hair was red like Evy's. It was Bowen.

"We have to get you out of here! Before the guards get back!" Buddy yelled, between the thunderous booms above.

Big Papa smiled. "Please do, but in the meantime hand me my granddaughter."

Buddy placed Evy atop the card table and began searching for the keys to the cell door. Big Papa laid his burly farm hands on Evy's face. His hands glowed blue and Evy's hair began to rise into the air, thick with electricity.

Evy's cold poisoned mind began to think. It was a painful low dud at first, a slow throbbing realization of the poison moving throughout her blood stream. She was weak from lack of food and her limbs were sore. She began to feel it all now, and she screamed out in pain. The noise of her screams was drowned, however, by the thunder above.

Big Papa's face contorted in intense concentration. He gripped her face harder, muffling the screams that were still coming from Evy's pained throat. Evy felt the poison begin to seep out slowly from her body. It poured like sticky ooze from her pores. She stopped screaming and opened her eyes slowly taking in her surroundings and then rose from the table. Strings of poisoned ooze hung from her body like sticky webs. Her large honey eyes looked around her, frightened and confused. Her body felt completely healed, even her hunger was gone.

Big Papa collapsed, weakened, onto the sewer floor. Bowen ran to him and cradled his head. He looked at Buddy desperately. "He could die," he said in whispers. Big Papa moaned and rolled to his side. "It takes a lot of his power away to heal someone. He hardly does it anymore, especially if it's been days that the person was sick. He's so old that it takes most of his healing powers just to keep him alive. If he uses them for someone else, his old organs begin to shut down."

"Is he going to be alright?" Buddy asked.

Clarence hugged Evy's leg under the table. Bowen shook his head yes. "His power will come back and heal him. It is just a painful process and he risks dying, too, if his organs fail before his trigger comes back."

Buddy sighed, deeply relieved.

"Where am I?" Evy asked.

Clarence still clung to her leg, as Evy stood. Buddy searched the table, the floor and the walls again for the key. An old woman with one eye shouted for him to look at a hook below one of the sconces and there they were — the keys. Buddy unlocked the gate and the people poured out. Bowen lifted Big Papa up off the floor and put his arm around him to steady him.

"The guards will be back. We need to stick together!" Buddy led the pack of dirty prisoners down the tunnel. He was not sure how to get out, but he hoped to get lucky. Evy and Clarence walked at the back of the pack with Bowen and Big Papa. Evy smiled up at Big Papa and took his hand, "Thank you," she whispered. "You, too, Clarence," she said, patting the skunk on the top of his head. Clarence stood taller beside her and puffed out his chest.

Big Papa finally introduced Bowen to his big sister (who just happened to be much younger). They marched through the tunnels together, arm in arm, in hopeful silence.

CHAPTER 16:
THE LIPPOLIK WAR

Fluffy, the pigeon, had gotten to Lady K in record time. Myra had told him how urgent the message was and he knew that those two humans were in a lot of trouble.

Lady K was beyond worried when Fluffy appeared in her window in the early evening hours. He had flown so hard to get there that he had lost quite a few feathers.

Lady K did not speak Fluffy, but she knew that if Myra had released him then they were in trouble, and she knew exactly where to look for trouble…Kallon.

Lady K gathered her rebels together and headed out to save Myra and Evy. Fluffy led them towards the scene of the kidnapping, but on their way, they ran into a weary, frazzled Myra and Doctor Bagby, who were on their way to get Kyla.

Myra told Kyla everything that had transpired during the last few days including where Kallon was hiding. Together, they all headed for Kallon's black tower.

Myra was able to find her way to the black tower by following Rufus. He had stupidly led her right to it. The place was heavily guarded, though, so that was when she had decided to go back and get reinforcements.

Kyla and Myra reached the tower with their band of rebels at exactly the right time. They arrived, bearing down on Kallon with fury. Kyla's timing could not have been more perfect for Buddy and Clarence. The storm that Lady K triggered was the perfect distraction for the guards in the tunnel dungeon. Her wrath at Kallon's horrible actions was hurricane-worthy and he had had it coming a long while.

Kallon saw his mother and her band of misfits arrive from his cozy, bedroom window. He felt the powerful storm begin to roar! He knew he was in trouble. So, he did the proper king thing and hid in the closet.

Below him, Kyla stood feet apart and anchored with her back arched towards the sky. Her black hair was blowing loose around her determined face. She raised her arms above her head and swirled the clouds with her mind. They turned black and heavy. A large cone of wind began to dip at the base of them and then it dropped like a heavy hammer on Kallon's beloved, black tower.

The building shuddered violently and the windows were blown out by the force of the hurricane's powerful winds. Rain poured down in heavy, stinging sheets. The sheer magnitude of the hurricane frightened the pirates and they were afraid to go outside and face the storm.

Rufus and Gracie rushed up the stairs to find the King. They searched everywhere in Kallon's room and finally found him curled up in his closet, sucking his thumb. Rufus drug him out of the closet by his foot and they all fought their way into the main hallway against the strong winds that had already claimed the windows and furniture.

Kallon seemed to compose himself in their presence. His resolve, albeit a bad one, was lifted when evil was around him. He clung to evil's horrid hand and mustered his courage enough to rally the Snake Pirates to their posts as he passed them on every floor.

Kallon now descended the steps with a whole army of angry Snake Pirates behind him. He knew that if they could make it to the sewer tunnels that all he would have to do was wait out the storm. He knew his mother's powers were not infinite, his own were not either. When she tired, they would have to fight.

He really did not want to, but it was inevitable. Their sordid relationship had always been on a collision course and besides, she had always liked Bowen best anyway.

Kallon stopped by the treasury room and grabbed his box of cursed, family jewels. Jack was already there, packing his share of jewelry into a large bag. He waved goodbye with a smirk on his face, and then, disappeared.

Kallon expected nothing less of Jack. He teleported back home, perhaps. Jack was a loner; he held alliance with no man. Kallon had left him alone in his solitude in exchange for help finding family members and their jewelry. He had been collecting them in hopes that he might gain their powers for himself. Jack had just handed them over to their doom without a thought.

But unfortunately, Kallon learned that once their powers were given the first time they were touched, the jewelry became like a magnet; it polarized itself to have the opposite effect. His studies of the jewelry had led him to the conclusion that they would protect him from everyone else's terrible triggers, but not give those same triggers to him.

It was for that reason; he began to adorn himself with every piece in the box. He threw them on carelessly. Draping and clipping them on himself anywhere he found space. Rufus watched him in his desperate endeavor and fingered the brooch that was still in his pocket. He had considered giving it back, but Myra was always mad at him. He had decided it was best to keep it. He hated being a possum and was determined to stay human from now on.

The storm outside was raging wildly and the building was falling down around them. Large bits of metal and wood crashed all around them. A metal support beam fell down on the troop of pirates and three were crushed. Kallon's eyes gazed at their broken bodies in disgust. How dare they die on him right now, when he needed them most! He draped one more gold, glittery necklace with a strange pendant around his neck, and then, began down the stairs again.

They reached the door to the sewer dungeon below them. It was a solid oak door with steps made of concrete descending to the dark tunnels below. There were six deadbolts on its surface so Kallon could sleep sound at night, coward that he was.

Kallon ordered the majority of his pirates to go out in the storm and fight. His army, numbering in the hundreds, poured out of the pane less doors and into the torrential storm to face the rebels. Kallon chose his six best guards to stay with him.

Meanwhile, Rufus decided that he had no intention of facing Myra; he would rather come back when the fighting was over and Myra was gone. He snuck away from the troupe of pirates and Kallon and went out the back door. Gracie saw him go, but she just rolled her eyes at him and ignored his cowardly way.

She was super glad that she was no longer tied to him, now that he was human. She had never really cared for him, anyway, and he always stunk terribly.

Kallon fumbled for his keys to unlock the door to the dungeon, the building was collapsing around him. Large, concrete blocks were beginning to fall around their heads now. The door was finally opened just as the ceiling began to give way.

The pirates that stayed with Kallon shoved and trampled each other to get into the door. Kallon, with all his heavy jewelry, was thrown against the wall and all but smashed to bits. The pirates charged ahead into the dark, abyss tunnels below.

Kallon peeled his sore body from the wall and descended wearily down the steps behind them. Ahead of him, the light from the wall sconces lit up the tunnel. Kallon could see people moving down the tunnel in shadows. He ordered his guards to halt, but they rushed forward in a panic to escape the rubble. Kallon saw the prisoners, from his dungeon, charge forward towards his pirates. He grabbed Gracie's arm and ducked into the tunnel beside him. Kallon and Gracie ran, his collection of jewelry clinking together loudly as he went and echoing off the sewer walls.

The Snake Pirates hit the crowd of prisoners head on. The dirty, ill-treated prisoners were all too happy to fight back.

Buddy grabbed a torch from the wall and began swinging it at the pirates, knocking them down in fiery blazes. A few other prisoners grabbed loose bricks shook free from the storm, or whatever else they could find to pound the pirates with. Evy morphed into a griffin and joined the fight. Only Clarence, Bowen and Big Papa stayed behind. Bowen laid Big Papa on the ground and held Clarence's gaze. "I trust you to keep him safe. If anyone comes at him, you scratch their eyes out. Got it?" Clarence nodded, enthusiastically.

Bowen stood and searched for a clear view. His triggering emotion was loving protection. He felt it now pulsing strongly in his heart, and throbbing through his veins. His eyes turned from blue to yellow. He raised his hands to hover horizontally over the tunnel floor. Then he began to pull at something imagined in his mind, up from the ground. His muscles strained with their imaginary load.

Large, thick vines began to grow from the sewer floor. Bowen closed his eyes and became one with the vines, melded with them; his body was physically sucked into their fibrous depths. He was a part of the plant now. He grew his tendrils out and wound his leafy arms around each of the six pirates, squeezing them tight. The prisoners stopped fighting and stood staring in amazement at their now tied up combatants. The pirates struggled in vain against their living bindings.

Bowen grew in length filling up the sewer with his plant-encased body. His tendrils budded and grew yellow flowers, which then, swelled into sweet fruits. He carried the pirates wound tightly in his vines down the sewer tunnels and into the jail cell that he and Big Papa once occupied. Bowen threw them inside and locked the gate.

He shuddered and stepped back, untangling his body and leaving behind the shelter of the monstrous plant he had created. He looked at it with pride, as his eyes slowly turned back to their normal sky blue color. He whispered to the plant in wind-like tones.

The plant listened to him and grew roots into the floor. It pushed its way through the sewer ceiling. Bricks tumbled and dirt collapsed as the cloudy, black sky peered through.

The prisoners had followed him back through the tunnel. They now climbed up the plant's giant trunk to the open rainy sky above.

Big Papa was still weak, but was on his feet with assistance now. His triggers were returning. Evy held his hand as they approached Bowen's plant. Big Papa shook his head disapprovingly, and then, punched Bowen hard on the arm.

"We've been imprisoned for years and you couldn't have done that a long time ago." Bowen rubbed his bruised arm and smiled.

"Kallon never hurt you the whole time we were here. My trigger is protection. I tried to use it against him when he came for you at the farm, but he had stolen my bracelet, it protected him from me. It weakened my power. I'm sorry."

Big Papa shrugged and began to climb the plant towards freedom. Evy hugged Bowen and then climbed up as well. Outside the storm was calming. The once grand tower Kallon had called home was now a massive pile of rubble and black, broken glass. As Evy climbed through the broken ceiling, she saw a huge army of animals in front of her. The P.B.U. had come to join the war.

Rufus stood in front of them triumphantly. His arms outstretched in a sarcastic welcoming gesture. Myra's purple, amethyst brooch glittered brilliantly as it lay in his outstretched hand. The prisoners huddled together behind Big Papa and Bowen for protection.

Evy felt her body shaking and morphing again. She hated Rufus. Her red feathers began to pop through her hair. She was weary from fighting, however, and the change was too slow. She had turned animal just enough, however, to hear a small Chihuahua in the front of the pack calling her name. It was the Chihuahua with the green paws and purple butt. She barked a soothing speech to Evy's tired ears. Rufus could no longer hear her animal words, now that he was human, but Evy understood!

The feathers fell from her head, drifting down in swirling circles to the rain-soaked ground. The animals were not here to hurt them. The Chihuahua was in control now. She had been able to win the war against Myra. Things would be set right once again.

Rufus laughed with his deep booming laugh. "I, Rufus Ignacio Phillips, win! The King will be pleased! Surrender, all you traitors to the King and we will hurt you less. Join me, my animal friends, in crushing our enemies. Let us destroy these friends to Myra, our destroyer, in the name of the King."

"If we win, he will turn you back to human, just as he's done for me. I brought him Evy, and behold, he gave me back my life. He is truly a magnificent King!" Rufus pointed his bony finger at the prisoners and screamed, "Charge!"

No one moved. The animals stood solid and still. Rufus stood frozen to his resolve and pointing a bony finger heinously into the empty air. He looked confused by the stillness behind him.

The green-pawed Chihuahua saw her chance and quickly jumped into the air, grasping the brooch from Rufus' outstretched hand in her teeth. She began to morph and change in midair. When she landed onto the ground, she was fully human. She looked exactly as her picture in Myra's family portrait book. Evy gasped, because Evelyn Lippolik stood tall and graceful before them. She looked from Rufus' dumbstruck face to the animal pack standing behind him. When she spoke, both Rufus and the P.B.U. understood.

"You are the traitor! You knew that this brooch could save us and you kept it to yourself. I saw you kill Dan the Pig in the P.B.U. yard! I saw you untie Myra and let her go! Myra is my sister and a kind soul deep down. I forgive her. She lost this brooch long ago, or she would have changed you all back and me, too. All of us, except for you, Rufus. Murdering, it seems, is in your blood. She changed you, because you murdered my husband!"

"NO! Myra killed Dan the pig, not me. Dan was my friend and colleague, why would I do that?" But Rufus' eyes betrayed his deceit. "I saw Myra do it!" He looked around desperately at the animal's glaring faces. He did not deny murdering Evelyn's husband, though, and that little omit was as good as a confession to the others.

His voice became more high-pitched and desperate. He saw that he was losing his grip on them. "The King needs you as you are fellow beasts and spies! Your reward is to be his humble servants for all time! It is the greatest of rewards!"

"This brooch is proof that you never intended to save us and that you are a liar. You kept it for yourself. You all saw it change me. Come touch it and your life will be restored." Evelyn held the brooch out to the animals.

Rufus's features became twisted in rage. He lunged at Evelyn, knocking her off her feet to the ground. "I should have killed you, too! I enjoyed watching your husband die and now I will get to watch you die as well. Dan was just collateral damage. He just knew too much."

Bowen stepped forward from the crowd of prisoners. He had another trigger, one that he never used — one that would make Rufus pay forever, without killing him. His protective love trigger was growing stronger for his grandmother and his heart began to pump and throb. He stretched out his hands and felt the power grow within him. His eyes turned yellow again.

Rufus stopped fighting with Evelyn as his body began to grow stiff and rigid. He could not move his arms and he began to panic, flailing them stiffly from side to side. His spine snapped to straight attention and his legs snapped straight as well. His toes began to grow longer as they tore out of his shoes and buried themselves in the dirt. He grew longer and taller. His gray, silver hair turned into shimmering leaves. His body was slowly encased by bark, and a dull, gray tree with shiny leaves stood tall before them all with two shocked-looking knotholes for eyes.

The P.B.U. gasped in shock. It was one thing to be turned into an animal, but a tree was insane. They decided to keep their eyes peeled for Bowen from now on. He was not to be crossed.

Evelyn lifted her slender frame off the ground and held the brooch out again towards the P.B.U. Clarence dove from atop Evy's shoulder at the brooch. He twisted and changed when his fingers touched it into a fairly, handsome young man, the same age he was when he was changed to a skunk. He looked very preppy and neat. His black hair was slicked down and parted in the middle and he wore an ugly, white sweater vest.

"Woohoo! I'm a man again!" To everyone's surprise, he had a British accent.

Twinkle and Bob, the mice, were the first members of the P.B.U. to crawl forward to touch the brooch. They were excited to be human again. Their jobs as Myra's mediocre and annoying cable guys had quickly become the hardest lesson that they ever learned. From now on they vowed to be the best at whatever they did.

The black horse was next. Her singing, long ago, was so horrible that it had annoyed Myra one day. Next, were the three Snake Pirate sheep (the largest of them still had a twitchy back leg), then the fence-jumping guy turned kangaroo bartender, the nasty neighbor who kept his house a mess turned pig, and so on and so on. Till at long last, everyone was human again. Suddenly, the P.B.U. had lost its purpose. They looked around unsure of what to do next. There was a lot of shoulder shrugging and empty stares. Myra had changed them into animals, but the King had taken everything else away.

Behind the mountainous rubble of Kallon's tower; Kyla, Myra, Bagby and the Rebels still fought the pirates. The building was gone, but the fight had just begun. They had no idea that the P.B.U.'s fighting was about to be over and that Rufus would soon be a tree.

The storm raged on. The rain and lightning beat at the pirates. The rebels fought valiantly and with conviction. The pirates were outnumbered and out-hearted. They were quickly subdued and the few that were not tied up, retreated in fear. Kallon and Gracie were swiftly all that was left of a once horribly powerful empire.

Kallon sat shivering and jingling loudly in his dark tunnel, afraid to face so many alone. Gracie sat in silence, listening to her headphones. She cared not how it all turned out. She did not care about much actually and that was her greatest flaw, complacency. She was just as guilty as Kallon, because she did nothing. Her lack of moral value and common decency were enough to make any judge and jury lock her up as well.

Myra looked at the giant pile of rubble and her heart sank. She charged forward towards the ruined remains. No one followed her, they stayed together and watched, but she did not care. The rebels were busy tying up the last of the Snake Pirates.

She began digging into the pile of glass, cutting her hands terribly. She was afraid that Evy or someone else might still be trapped inside. Tears of fear rolled down her face and she continued digging. She found a man hole beneath a pile of glass and dropped down inside it. Kyla watched from the arms of Charlie the rifleman. She was too weary to follow after her, because of the hurricane so she stayed behind with her troops, but went with her in spirit.

The tunnel was black as pitch. The torches were either blown out, or extinguished from the steady drips of rain leaking in. She walked slowly on, searching the darkness with strained eyes. Behind her Charlie the rifleman dropped down inside the tunnel, too. He patted her back and they walked in together.

"Hello! Anyone alive down here?" Myra called out. No one answered. They turned right and continued walking a bit, then left. A flight of concrete stairs led upwards to their left. The floor at the foot of the stairs was covered in debris. A fight had taken place there, no doubt.

Charlie nodded, cocked his gun and they ascended the stairs. The top of the stairs was blocked off by wreckage, but there was a tunnel running to the right. She could hear a clinking sound coming from its depths. They stepped lightly into it and followed its curves into the darkness.

Kallon heard the gun cocking echo in the darkness. He and Gracie stood up and pressed their bodies flat against the rough, brick walls. It was too dark to see. "Hello?" Myra called again. At the sound of her voice, Kallon recognized Myra and if he knew his Aunt Myra, which he did, she was probably alone. His confidence grew and he began to wet his mouth with sticky, poisoned saliva. It was the advantage of him having a wicked tongue.

Gracie closed her eyes and turned her head. She turned the volume up on her ipod. She hated seeing her family die, but she did not care really. Kallon crouched and stretched out his gummy arms. He pulled them out longer and longer. Fear was his trigger, ironically, and he was afraid. Then he grabbed Gracie's ankles, setting a trap that would trip Myra if she walked their way. They waited with bated breath.

Myra and Charlie began to feel a bit afraid, too. Myra's hairs on the back of her neck stood with electricity. She stepped with caution. Charlie stopped close to the entrance and pointed his rifle into the empty, black air. As soon as he did, Myra tripped on something. Her body flew, and her legs kicked madly in midair. She landed with a bump!

Kallon took his opportunity to jump on Myra. He sat on top of her stomach and prepared to hock poisoned saliva into her pretty face. Myra's arms crackled with electricity and Kallon let go with a yelp. He spit into the random air where it fizzled and was swallowed by the thirsty, dry sewer earth. Charlie saw a figure in the glow of sudden electricity sitting on top of Myra. He shot at it and missed as the tunnel fell black once again. The bullet ricocheted off the bricks and hit Gracie in the leg. She fell screaming to the ground in pain.

"Kallon, give up and come home. We want you to be with us, not against us!" Myra pleaded, but Kallon prepared to spit at her again.

"Noooooooo!" Myra stammered. She felt her trigger begin to rise as the air grew hot with electricity. Gracie felt it, too. Charlie stepped further back in the tunnel towards the stairway to escape the electrical heat.

Her trigger began to take over her and before she could get hold of herself, CRACK! A large boom shook the tunnel walls and blew the lid off the manhole.

Myra's worst trigger had done its best, once again.

Myra lit her hands with purple electricity so she could see in the dark and search through the massive pile of jewelry for a purple-butted beast. She found nothing. Gracie was gone, too. She searched for minutes on end afraid to give up, but she did not feel anything but metal.

Evy's feather bracelet lay on the top of the pile of jewelry. Myra picked it up and put it in her pocket. Then she slunk solemnly out of the tunnel. Her head was hung in shame.

How was she going to tell Kyla? Charlie was waiting for her at the bottom of the stairs. "What happened? Are you okay?" he asked. "Whatever it was, whatever happened, I know it was self-defense." Myra shook her head unwilling to speak. She felt awful. They climbed out of the tunnels and joined the troupe of rebels. Myra kept her eyes shamefully on the ground.

Meanwhile, deep in the tunnel, the pile of jewelry began to quiver and shake. Long, hairy legs poked through the entangling jewels. A large fist-sized hairy body wiggled its way out and a purple-butted spider, the first of his kind, appeared. The jewelry's combined power had actually sucked Myra's powers into him.

Beside him, a black crow with a purple-butt and a bleeding leg looked at him with her very, shiny eyes and screamed. Far away down the tunnel, the six pirate prisoners heard the horrifying scream and hid in the corner of their prison chamber in silence, because they were suddenly unable to speak. The spider emerged and pulled a large green ring off his leg. He placed it onto his head like a crown. His reign would now begin as Kallon, the Spider King.

CHAPTER 17:

BLACK GLASS MOUNTAIN

Evy walked around the black mountain of glass, and saw her mom. Behind her, Kyla saw her mom, too, for the first time in thirty-five years. Evelyn and Evy ran to Kyla and they hugged. Myra watched them saddened and unexpectedly lonely. Bagby saw her face turn melancholy and laid his giant nose on her shoulder, which she quickly brushed away. Big Papa and Bowen joined in the family embrace. Then Big Papa walked over to Myra and hugged her, also. Myra pretended to just endure it, with her arms held stiffly to her sides, but her heart inside was full. His warm embrace comforted her.

The confused P.B.U. members walked around the rubble, too. Myra jumped backwards at the sight of them and her hair flew statically around her face. She lifted her arms karate-style, and her fingers sparkled with purple lightning. Gus the Armadillo, who had been in charge of spying on Myra, stepped forward. He waved his arms in surrender.

"Please calm down, Myra. We don't want to be turned into animals, yet again. I forgive you...kind of. I guess what I mean to say is that I want peace. I'm tired and old. I've spent so much time on revenge and now I just want peace. Let's just go our separate ways and let bygones be bygones, shall we? I have one demand, however. You better pin that brooch to your skin, because if you turn another person, I'll come looking for you."

With that, the P.B.U. walked away forever. They followed Gus like sheep into the shadows of the broken city, their human lives at last regained. They were, unfortunately, unsure of what to do with them though.

"Eehum!" Bagby cleared his donkey throat. His eyes were glued to the brooch in Evelyn's hand.

"Oh, yes, of course. Myra, here. You do the honor, please." Evelyn handed the brooch to Myra.

Myra looked at it glimmering softly in her hand, the key to all her troubles. "I'm sorry, Evelyn. You know I didn't mean to." Myra and Evelyn embraced.

"I know you didn't. You still owe me big time, but thanks for helping me raise Kyla." Evelyn smiled.

Myra cleared her throat, "I'm so sorry, Bagby. I never meant to hurt you, or anyone. I promise to give you any cures you may ever need from now on. I hope that you can forgive me in time and that we might work together to cure the world."

She touched his hairy side with the brooch. Bagby shivered and shook. He twisted and morphed. He changed before them into a fat doctor in tight, black leotards wearing white doctor's shoes. Everyone gasped, and then, started laughing hysterically.

"It's a long story!" he said, grinning at them with embarrassment under his gray, walrus mustache.

Clarence walked around the crowd and over to Myra. He popped an old mint into his mouth, which he found in his pocket from his college years. It was something he should have done a long time ago. Then to everyone's surprise, he kissed Myra square on the lips.

She was shocked at first, and then, she slapped him hard in the face. Clarence stepped back and squeezed his eyes closed. He waited with teeth gritted, for his return to skunk form. "It was worth it," he mumbled.

Myra stared at him with a smirk on her face. Clarence slowly opened one eye. "That wasn't half bad, Clare. You should have done that, years ago." Clarence smiled and leaned in for another. "I don't think so," Myra said, shoving him hard in the chest.

Evy eyed Big Papa from across the crowd. He was still leaning heavily on Bowen. She wondered again if he felt responsible for this whole mess. He had to be the source of the mysterious, birthday jewelry. If he was, she had to know. She loved him so much and could not bring herself to believe that he would put the world in danger like that. Evy pushed through the people towards him. Big Papa caught her eye as she parted the crowd.

"Big Papa, I have a question for you," she whispered in his ear and she grabbed him by the arm. Big Papa looked confused.

"Why would you send me that bracelet? Why would you send Kallon a piece of magic jewelry, too, when you knew what he was like as a child? Why would you give him the power to destroy the country?"

Big Papa shook his head. "It wasn't me. I keep telling everyone that. I've tried to stop this from happening. I don't know where she is." He began to cry. Small plants began to bud from his tears on the ground.

"Where, who is?" Evy asked confused.

"You wouldn't believe me even if I told you. It's a very, long story."

"Please, I have to know. We can't let these kinds of things keep happening."

He looked up at her; his budding trees were now at chin height. Evy smiled back at him, encouraging him. The crowd behind her got quiet, suddenly aware of their conversation.

"Her name is Delilah. She is the Queen of the Leprechauns. Oh, yeah, and she hates me."

It took a moment to sink in, and then, Evy laughed. "Obviously she does, and lately, I would believe anything. I'll help you find her. We have to stop her and find a way to make ourselves normal again." Big Papa nodded in agreement.

And that was the beginning of the beginning of a new life for everyone. It was definitely not the end, though. Kyla, or Lady K, became the leader of the "New America" as it was called. She married Charlie.

Then together, with Big Papa and Bowen's help, they regrew America's plant life. Without the poisoned saliva consistently being pumped in, the rivers and lakes cleaned themselves eventually. It turned out that it only took a tiny drop to poison a whole river. Once the poison bonded with the water, it grew like a giant sponge until it had choked out all wildlife and was too thick to enter the roots of plants.

Myra went back to her solitude, but stayed close by. She never told Kyla what happened with Kallon and Kyla never asked. She had no idea that Myra was the reason Kallon was gone. Kyla felt like it was her fault and the mother part of her did not want to know what had happened. Besides, Lippoliks do not pry.

Bagby set up a doctor's office near the school house and became the town physician. Every once in a while, he would visit Myra for a major cure, but mostly he cured things the old fashioned way. Clarence continued to stalk Myra. Only she let him, most of the time.

Evy was happy to have her simple life back for awhile. Enjoying her family was all she ever wanted to begin with. The search for Delilah the Leprechaun Queen was imperative though. Evy would begin planning a search with Big Papa, Myra and Bowen, but that is a tale for another time.

ABOUT THE AUTHOR
KAMI HELM

Kami was born in Longview, Texas and spent most of her childhood in rural parts of Texas. She grew up as an artist specializing in cartoons and obtaining a degree in Art History. She now spends her time as a full time novelist and stay-at-home mom to three children. Her husband, Jeremy, is also an artist and did all the design work for her book and website.

Inspired by her adventures in the woods as a child, she began writing The Lippolik Conundrum. Writing was always a childhood dream of hers and she was greatly encouraged by her mother, who is an accomplished writer as well.